OUTLAW

Viking Ventures - Book 2

Ole Åsli
Tony Bakkejord

Envig AS

ENVIG
FORLAG

ISBN: 978-82-93794-92-9 (e-book)
ISBN: 978-82-93794-91-2 (paperback)
ISBN: 978-82-93794-90-5 (hardcover)

Cover design by: Gamst Design
Library of Congress Control Number: 2018675309
Paperback and hardcover editions printed in the United States of America

Ui Néill
Ulaid
Oriel
Breifne
Glyde
Linn Duachaill
Blackwater
Kells
Meath
Boyne
Connacht
Boyne
Liffey
Dyflin
Leinster
Osraige
Munster

CHAPTER 1: ALONE

Meath, Ireland, October 841

Ulv opened his eyes and screamed.

The hoarse outcry turned into a coughing fit. His chest burned as if splattered with glowing coals. His mouth and throat were scraped raw. Dark, clotted blood covered his torso, with paler streaks where fresh blood still flowed from the two cuts.

Ulv wanted to touch his chest, rub his eyes. But he could not. His hands were tied behind the tree. He had to concentrate on feeling anything but pain and moved his fingers and toes to check that they were still functioning. His wrists were aching; his arms were numb. His legs pricked and throbbed.

Ulv closed his eyes to see more clearly.

The ship that slid across the water towards the village in Northumbria. The scent of salt water and wet sand. Kjetil Korte who shouted at him. The old man who died with the knife in his gut. The warmth from the sticky blood all over his hand. The stench of damp soil and sour smoke in the cellar where Marcus sat wide-eyed and terrified. The duel with Kjetil. The voyage where two of Geir Galne's berserks died after challenging Magnus Trygg. The cold wind at the Orkneyar where he had fought Kjetil again. And where he had tried to find Marcus's sister. The dread at the top of the cliff he climbed with Vass.

He recalled the attack on Dyflin. Vass armed with a pitchfork with two spikes and Ulv with the bow. The men he had fought. Those he had killed. He saw himself within the palisade with Vass and recollected the agreement with the Irish chief.

The deal that saved many and killed others. Aud, the volve, who demanded that the Irish embrace Odin to live. The girl who cried and repeated the words that Aud commanded but who died anyway. The young man with the stern visage who escaped. He remembered the arrow he had aimed at the Irishman, but that he never released. The logs on the river that moved when he jumped. He felt the warmth of the recognition when he was the first to cross. The fear when Kjetil appeared in Dyflin.

He remembered the sight of the giant's broken nose. The joy when Kjetil told him that Marcus was behind it. The despair when Flatnose demanded that Ulv would take the punishment for his thrall.

Ulv had said goodbye to Vass, left Dyflin and gone out into the wilderness. Alone. An outcast. An outlaw. And so very afraid.

Ulv opened his eyes wide. The men who had attacked him while he was sleeping! He tried to lift his head and look around. It did not take long before everything moved again.

He forced his head up, but it was too much. Too early.

His head fell forward, and his eyes slid shut.

*

Ulv opened his eyes.

He looked at the destruction. At the creatures that worked frantically. As if they did not realise that it was useless. They swarmed around without meaning. Ulv wondered if they screamed in fear. If they howled in grief. If they groaned in pain. He wondered if anyone was trying to run away. If anyone was hiding? How many were killed? How many had lost family members?

Somebody was lying in a pool of blood. His blood. It flowed like a lazy autumn stream down his thigh, on the side of his knee and stopped at his calf. In this red pool, he saw shapes. Three young men with arrows protruding from their bodies. An old man with a gaping wound in his stomach and dark eyes.

Ulv shook his head. Tried to clear his mind.

They were ants. Ants examining his blood. Ants swarming around. Most were gathered around his legs protruding from the anthill.

There was no panic. They were not powerless. They had meaning. A goal. Maybe there still was something that could be done?

Maybe it was not too late.

Ulv stretched his arms up by the trunk behind him. Fortunately, there were no branches at the bottom of the tree. It also helped that he had tightened his muscles when they tied him up. He managed to get his arms a hand's breadth further up. Then another. But then they stopped. Despite being flexible, he could not get any further. He rested, knowing that he would only get this one chance. His energy drained with the blood flowing from the red cross over his chest. He planned his next movements. Envisioned the steps to get free. It gave him strength to have a goal. A meaning. To get his arms further up, he leaned forward and heaved them up the trunk. The rough trunk scraped at his arms.

He breathed. Rested.

One last time.

A few deep breaths. He pulled his legs from the anthill, pressed his back against the tree trunk and lifted his feet in front of him. His stomach tightened, and before he could get his legs all the way up over his head, fresh blood trickled from the cuts on his chest. He squeezed his ankles around the tree above and turned his head to the side of the trunk. Hanging there, he breathed for a moment. Holding his weight with his feet, he could drag his arms and the rope further up. Repeating the process, he climbed the tree a few inches at a time.

Again and again he dragged himself upwards. He was dizzy, and it felt like his shoulders were going to pop out of their sockets. A little more. One of his feet touched something. A branch. He groaned and lifted his feet over it. Rest. The rope was slack behind the trunk now. Could he reach the knot with his fingers? Almost. Moving his arms a little further up, he grabbed the knot and forced himself to feel the shape of it before he started pulling at some of the parts.

The world rocked. There was no more time. He pulled on one of the rope arches. It came loose. Desperate, he continued pulling.

The knot came loose. He fell. Thudding to the ground, darkness found him.

*

Ulv awoke. His mouth was dry as ash, and he ached everywhere. Apart from his undergarments, he was naked. For a while, he just lay there, trying to remember what had happened. The tip of the knife that was pulled over his chest. The brown stumps of teeth and the man who owned them. The pieces fell into place. The bloody cuts across his chest ached and were stiff, but they did not bleed much anymore. He suspected that would change as soon as he started moving. It did not matter. He had to get up and about. Carefully he sat up and looked around. The anthill was ruined. His right foot was still in the hill, and the furious workers fought to chase the intruder away. Ulv pulled his foot out and brushed away the insects. It stung and burned from countless minor wounds.

There was moss nearby, of the type Father said would protect wounds from festering. He got up and loosened the piece of rope that still hung in the tree. Unbraiding it, he loosened the thin threads the rope was made of. After collecting the moss, he laid it over the wounds and tied the cords around his upper body to hold it in place. He had not taken twelve steps before he realised that the moss would not stay in place for long. Still, it was the best he could do.

Ulv went to the stream he had found the day before. The water was cold and fresh, and he drank greedily. The sun was at its highest, which meant that half a night and half a day had passed since the thugs assaulted him. Ulv intended to get his revenge. He would never forget the feeling of being awakened by blows and kicks. Of five men standing over him, with cold smiles and weapons in hand. He would take revenge for the fear he had felt, for the pain he had suffered. For the pain he still suffered. Most of all, he would avenge the feeling of security they had knocked out of him. That last remnant of safety he had felt alone in the woods.

They had taken his equipment as well. Without it, he would not survive. Revenge may not be the most important thing. But it should be possible to kill two crows with one arrow. Then he remembered the bow and the other equipment he had pushed under the rock. Had the thugs taken it? The urge to find out if he still had a weapon took over as the most critical need, and he got up from the creek. The dizziness returned in full when he stood upright, and he had to lean on a tree not to fall. He staggered back towards the campsite. On the way, he picked up some large leaves from a bog plant.

At the campfire, he slid down to his knees. The movement made him feel like an old man, watching his every move not to aggravate his pains. Bending down, he saw that the bow was still under the rock. The bowstring, the arrowheads, the feathers from the crow, and the axe were also there. But no clothes and no food. This meant that he had the most important things to carry out the plan, but nothing extra. The way forward was clear.

Most of the moss had come loose from his chest. He untied the threads, gathered new moss, put the large leaves over the moss and fastened it all over again with the cords. He gathered up what little remained of his equipment and followed the brigands' tracks.

Browntooth and his men had made no attempt to hide their tracks. Footprints in soft soil, bent heather and broken twigs made it easy for Ulv to follow. In the afternoon, the search was over, and he heard the men before he saw them. Sneaking, he approached their camp. The men talked and laughed. A dog barked. Then a loud voice and a bark that went over in a whimper.

Suddenly a man appeared, with his arms full of firewood. He was no more than fifteen steps away, and Ulv could do nothing but sit still and hope he was not discovered. The man turned and came straight towards where Ulv was seated. Taking hold of the axe, Ulv hunkered down. A confrontation would be catastrophic. Even if he managed to overcome the man, the others would come rushing in, and everything would be over. A few more steps, and the man would definitely see him.

Then the man stopped and bent down in front of a tuft. He picked up a stick and put it on top of the armful of logs. Turning, he went back to the camp. Ulv let out a breath he did not know he had held. His heart was pounding. He had to get ready.

Ulv turned and stole away. When he was sure the men could neither see nor hear him, he went a bit further. He found a bush with two straight branches. These would do for arrow shafts. Nearby he found two more. These were not as straight, but he did not take the time to look any further. The dizziness still plagued him, and he got tired of the slightest effort. Without clothes, food and rest, it would only get worse. He had to do this today.

According to his plan, he only needed one good arrow. Another three were barely usable. If he had more time, he could have straightened the crooked shafts. But then he had to heat them over a fire. There was no time for that. From a nearby tree, he carefully scraped off the bark on one side of the trunk and carved a herringbone-shaped scar in the trunk to drain the resin. He removed the bark on the shafts and straightened what he could with the axe. He sharpened one end so that the arrowheads could be fitted. It was not easy with only the axe to help him, but fortunately, it was sharp. Ulv sent his thanks to the man who owned the axe for taking such good care of the tool. It could very well save his life.

Then he made a notch in the other end of the arrows so that the string could fit. It took its time, and he had to cut one arrow a couple of times because the notch became too deep. Drops of sweat ran down his forehead when all four shafts had notches at the end. He began to twist the loose underbark into fine threads that he would use to tie up the feathers and ensure the arrows did not split at the notch. Shaping the feathers with nothing but an axe was tedious and frustrating work, but eventually he had a dozen curved steering feathers. He would prefer them to be longer but had to settle for what he got. The best arrow was fitted with the longest set of feathers.

Longer fletching makes the arrow stabilise faster in the air, but it loses speed quicker.

He could still hear Father's voice explaining the many details of the craft. At a short distance, long fletching was not a disadvantage.

He attached the feathers to the shafts with the resin that ran from the wound in the tree. Then he pulled the twisted threads through the resin before tying them around the shaft of the arrow. Finally, he tied some cords around the shaft where the notch stopped. The arrows were not a pretty sight, but they would do. Had to do. He was well pleased with the best one. It would do the job just fine. Ulv hoped he would not have to bet his life that the other arrows would work just as well.

The sun hung low in the sky when Ulv sneaked back towards the camp. For a moment, he wondered what people would think if they saw him. He must be a strange sight. Without shoes or clothes up to his hips, where he wore blood-stained undergarments. His upper body was covered with moss and large leaves, held in place by thin threads tied across his body. His face, which must have been pale, was smeared with mud. His hair was wet and sticking to his head. Sweat ran down his cheeks. In one hand, he carried a short bow, and in the other, he held four arrows. An axe was hooked into a piece of rope that served as a belt. He seemed like a madman. He felt like a madman.

The flickering light from the fire made it easy to find the camp. Even in the distance, he heard a voice that made his neck hairs stand on end. Browntooth. It was hard to breathe. His body was heavy, and it took all his concentration to move stealthily through the woods. He stopped behind a large tree. From there, he could hear the voices and glimpse men sitting around a fire. There were four of them. Ulv searched for the fifth man, at the same time as he hoped he would not find even more in the camp. Behind the four, he glimpsed a rocky hill or some large stones. There was a darker area, too. A cave entrance, perhaps? An old cart stood to the right of the campfire, and a tent to the left. Ulv stole a few steps closer. He had to finish this. He was running out of strength.

CHAPTER 2: LOOT

The sun was setting when Vass wandered in the gate at the fortified eastern part of Dyflin. Torgils had gathered the warriors to distribute the meagre loot after the raid. The Irish tended to hide their valuables in the monasteries, while there was little of worth where people lived. Dyflin was taken for strategic reasons. Some would argue that the booty gathered was as deplorable as the honour of capturing the village. There had been little actual fighting. Apart from the problem with those who had entrenched themselves within the palisades, the battle had been straightforward. Vass and Ulv had solved the problem by negotiating an agreement with a knife to the Irish leader's throat. Vass did not expect to be rewarded for it. Torgils had not been satisfied by Vass and Ulv negotiating on his behalf.

Despite the meagre spoils, the warriors were in good spirits. The tension and trepidation of battle abated, and they felt the genuine joy of being alive. Despite the festive mood of the group, Vass kept in the background. He did not know many of the gathered men. After climbing the Old Man of Hoy with Ulv, they were picked up by Ragnar and his crew of Danes. That was why Vass and Ulv had participated in the attack on Dyflin, while Geir Galne and the other berserks rowed up the River Boyne towards the monastery in Kells.

In any case, there was need getting in line first. It was a long time until it was his turn to choose from the pile of valuables.

Torgils and his entrusted housecarls stood laughing and toasting with drinking horns and silver mugs, turning their backs on everybody else. Veterans of countless battles, all were decorated with rings and jewellery. A couple of them had grown soft around their bellies, a sure sign they had spent more time celebrating their past victories than preparing for the next. One of them turned and met his gaze. Vass wiped away his grimace with his hand and shifted his gaze to a man standing on the outskirts of the group – a tall, slender man with broad shoulders. Olaf, Torgils's right-hand man.

Olaf stepped forward and proclaimed that Torgils would choose first, followed by Ragnar. Then he listed several names Vass did not know. The men around him glanced sideways at each other and frowned. It was not uncommon for men to feel overlooked in such contexts. Nothing, however, was said aloud, and soon Torgils stepped forward. The broad warrior had taken off the chain mail he had been wearing during the attack earlier in the day and was now wearing weapon shirt and green wool trousers. In his belt, he carried a seax hanging across his stomach but no sword. Like many of his men, he wore high leather boots instead of the more typical low shoes. He went straight to where some weapons were lined up against the wall of one of the buildings. He picked up a sword and held it up. 'I choose this sword, an Ulfberht blade from Saxony. The sharpest and strongest sword I have ever seen.'

Light reflected from the blade. The men around Vass mumbled. Vass went closer. More than a little interested in weapons, he wanted to take a closer look at the sword. Before he reached the front of the throng, Torgils had rejoined his flock of housecarls. Vass changed direction and walked towards the remaining weapons that were lined up along the wall. There was nothing of decent quality. Had he found the pitchfork there, the one with only two spikes, he would have taken it when it was his turn. But a broken farm tool had not been found worthy of a place among the spoils.

One by one, named warriors were called out. After Ragnar, many of Torgils's own men helped themselves to their share of the loot, and soon there remained little of value. After a while, Olaf took the floor and let the rest of the warriors come forward. The rabble. Vass did not bother to get to the front of the crowd. He was just about to walk away when he noticed a whetstone. His own had disappeared after they left Sanday, and he needed a new one.

'That's an Eidsborg whetstone,' said a grey-bearded warrior as Vass picked up and studied the stone. 'Best whetstone you'll get. Had I seen it, I would have taken it myself. I guess that is the greatest treasure here, after the sword.'

That said more about the loot than the whetstone. Still, Vass smiled at the man and thanked him. He withdrew from the crowd, spat on the light grey stone and tested it against the edge of his axe. After a few strokes on each side, he understood what the old man was talking about. The fine-grained stone was not fast to work with, but the edge definitely got sharper. He found a quiet place just outside the gates and sat down.

Vass had finished sharpening the axe and was working on his sword when he heard a child shouting. Glancing up, he saw one of Torgils's warriors pulling a woman away from a terrified boy of four or five winters. Vass had seen him before. A man with brown hair in a ponytail and a beard adorned with rings of silver showed a grey row of teeth when he snarled at the boy.

Vass rose and let go of his sword and whetstone. 'Let her go,' he said quietly.

The warrior stopped and looked up into the air before he turned to face the bothersome Dane. He pulled the woman closer and grabbed her tight around her waist.

'What did you say?' The man had an incredulous expression.

'I told you to let her go.'

'Don't meddle in the affairs of grown-ups, boy! Run away, before I give you a beating you will not soon forget!'

'Oh, I apologise, I thought you only fought women and

children,' Vass replied in a voice he could not keep quite steady.

'You bastard! I'll give you one last chance ... Get out of here before I break you like a dry twig!'

A handful of curious Northmen gathered around them, drawn by the expectation of a fight.

'Come on then, *gamling*! Show me you dare take on somebody your own size!' Vass wanted the assailant to let go of the woman and make the first move.

The warrior's eyes widened. He shoved the woman away and turned to Vass with clenched fists. Vass hoped for a quick and uncontrolled attack, but his opponent did not fall into that trap. Vass waited as the experienced fighter came closer with a devious smile on his face.

Five paces from Vass, he sprung into motion with fists flying. A quick jab, followed by a right hook, forced Vass to dodge and retreat two steps. But the warrior pressed on with another punch. This time, he put his weight behind it, and it was too close for Vass to evade. The Dane took a step to the right, caught the man's fist with his left hand and grabbed his shoulder with his right. The warrior lost his balance, and Vass forced him into the mud with his thumb pressing into the soft area between his foe's thumb and forefinger and his other hand's index and middle fingers pressing in between the shoulder and the chest muscle.

'Leave the woman and her boy alone,' Vass hissed as he bent down over his opponent.

'Mmmffffff!' was the only reply.

'I can't hear you!' Vass squeezed harder, forcing a stream of incomprehensible sounds and grunts from his victim.

'You'll stay far away from her!' Vass said, and eased his grip.

'Yes,' muttered the man.

Unconvinced, Vass tightened the grip again.

'Yes, I'll stay away! Just let me go!' the prone warrior cried.

Vass settled the argument and left his opponent in the mud.

The group of onlookers parted when Vass passed between them, staring straight ahead. He picked up his sword and whetstone and made his way out of the town.

Vass needed to clear his mind.

Outside of town, Vass sat with his eyes closed and concentrated on his breathing until his heartbeat slowed and his hands stopped shaking.

The Vikings would have their way with women and Vass could do little about it. That was not what triggered the reaction. He had lost his temper, and it was only luck that he had not beheaded the warrior. It was not even a conscious choice to leave his weapons behind when he confronted him. Vass got up and shook his head to get rid of the last remnants of the emotions that had flared up in him. He did not quite succeed.

There was something about the boy and his mother.

CHAPTER 3: WINE AND HONEY

Marcus awoke to the sound of rain. With his eyes closed, he lay still and listened, trying to force his body and brain to obey.

He was Marcus, son of Gaius, the merchant from Wucestre in Northumbria. *Or was he?*

Gaius was dead, killed by a slender Viking boy. Marcus was nobody's son anymore. He was all alone. *Where?* Opening his eyes, he looked up at the wooden boards. Planks, close together. Roof. To the left, the planks met a wall of stone and mortar. His gaze followed the wall and found an opening where light came in. A window, with glass.

Who can afford glass windows?

An indefinable sound to his right made him turn. On a table, an arm's length away from his bed, lay a man with leather straps tied to his wrists and ankles. Another band was strung over his forehead and a broader strap over his belly. Apart from a loincloth, the man was naked.

Marcus glanced down his own body and found that he had been allowed to keep his trousers. A grey woollen robe lay beside the bed. He pulled the robe over his head and got up to look at the man. His unfortunate guest had dark hair and beard, both cut short – unevenly so. A bloodied bandage covered his broad shoulders and chest. His breathing was laboured, and his skin glistened with sweat.

The wounded man was Bjarn, the Viking who sat by Marcus's side on the fateful journey up the Blackwater. Marcus was happy and surprised to see the Northman, but he doubted Bjarn would survive if he did not get help.

Marcus glanced around the small room. The bed he had been lying on was placed next to the wall by the window. Through the wet glass, he could glimpse a green meadow and a forest behind it. Their room was three to four man-lengths above ground level.

He walked across the room and tried to open the door. Something on the outside made it impossible to push it open. After knocking a few times without getting any response, he sat down on the bed and tried to remember what had happened the previous day.

His shoulders and arms started to ache as he realised he had rowed from morning to late evening. The memories of the attack on the ship came to him, along with his flight through the forest. He had stepped on Kjetil Korte's face, and he had helped Sigurd Jarl stay on his feet for long enough to kill two Irishmen, until a heavy spear ended his life. Marcus remembered kneeling and looking up at an old man who spoke to him. Accompanied by a dozen Irishmen, he had wandered through the night in heavy rain. Eventually, they passed through the gates of what had been their destination: the abbey of Kells.

Looking around the room once more, he tried to determine if he was a prisoner or a guest. He was not tied up and had no guard, at least not inside the room. But the door was barred, and he could not go anywhere. Bjarn had not been with the group going through the forest and would not have managed the trek by himself. Somebody must have carried him later. Maybe the Northmen had delivered him there to get help? Or had the Irish found him and allowed him to live?

In any case, something must be done about Bjarn's wound and fever. In a monastery, there had to be monks with knowledge of such things. Determined to get help, he returned to the door. He considered calling *help* but thought it would unsettle Bjarn if he revealed that he had no control over the situation. If the Northman was able to notice it at all.

He considered what else he could shout and rejected *fire*, *food* and *let me out* before he settled on *water.* It was a natural request under the circumstances. If he was lucky, somebody would interpret it to mean that an actual fire had to be extinguished. Satisfied that his language skills would once again come in handy, he decided to use Latin words, which priests and monks often understood.

'Aqua! Aqua!' he shouted, followed by three firm knocks on the door. He retreated a few steps and waited. Moments later, he heard footsteps on the stone floor outside. A bar was lifted away, and the door was opened by a middle-aged man in a brown robe. The monk had a high forehead, and his head was shaved in a wedge from ear to ear, leaving the back of his head hairless.

'Aqua,' Marcus repeated. The monk nodded and closed the door again. After a while, he returned with two jugs of water. 'Gratias,' said Marcus. The monk raised an eyebrow and replied: 'Gratias *tibi ago*,' emphasising the last two words. Marcus nodded, accepting the lesson.

When the monk turned to leave, Marcus put his hand on his shoulder to stop him. The monk stopped, looked down at his hand and brushed it away as if he chased away a fly. 'Ignosce!' Marcus said, when he recalled the Latin word for apology.

'Mihi. Ignosce mihi,' muttered the monk.

Marcus nodded again. 'Mihi,' he repeated. He pointed to Bjarn, wounded and feverish on the table, before he shrugged and showed his empty palms.

The monk replied by pointing at Marcus's chest.

Marcus shook his head and said, 'I know nothing about treating wounds', in his native language. The monk extended his arm further until he poked at Marcus's chest with his index finger. Then, he pointed straight up, said 'cum gratia dei,' and made the sign of the cross before he walked out the door.

Marcus was given responsibility for treating Bjarn himself. By the grace of God, of course. The monks figured the Northman would survive if God wanted it so. Otherwise, he would die, no matter how Marcus treated his wounds and fever. Apparently, Matthew's words about not tempting your god were not widely known among the Irish, but Marcus understood why they would not exert themselves to keep marauding heathens alive.

On the wall between the window and the door hung a long, narrow shelf with several objects on it: a shiny silver bowl of water, a short knife with a shaft of bone, and six small jars with a piece of cloth tied to the top of each. Two lit candles stood next to each other. By the door lay a stack of linen cloth, washed and folded.

Marcus removed the cloth from the jars and examined their contents. The alluring smell of honey from the first jar reminded him that it had been a long time since he had eaten. The last meal he remembered was on board the ship the previous afternoon. They had been attacked in the evening, and he had been walking for most of the night. Afterwards, he had slept for a long time. He hoped there was something good in the other jars as well, and preferably some bread somewhere.

The next two jars contained herbal poultices of some kind. One was light green, the other yellow. Marcus did not recognise the scent, and they did not fit in with the meal he had begun to envision. In the fourth jar, there was a liquid that smelled of sour wine. Marcus tasted it. The drink was strong and tasted awful.

Marcus was already upset about the Irish eating habits when he opened the fifth jar. It was half full of larvae. White, naked larvae, as long as his fingernail. He resealed the cloth to keep the larvae from crawling out. The sixth jar contained a thick liquid that formed a sticky coating. Marcus surmised that it must be animal fat. Herbs, honey, strong wine, animal fats and larvae. Those were not a meal, but remedies for healing wounds.

Marcus regretted that he had not learned how to treat a wound. There were several different approaches, but he knew not how to choose one over another. His mother believed in rinsing with clean water. It seemed reasonable enough, but she never explained the purpose. Some of the elderly women covered wounds with lards to keep the evil spirits from entering the body through the damaged skin. Of course, nobody mentioned such practices when there was a priest nearby. Some herbs were rumoured to prevent wounds from festering, while others helped against the fever. But Marcus did not know which herb worked for what.

Honey sped up the healing of wounds but was not helpful against fever or large amounts of pus. Manure was allegedly better under such circumstances. The wounds could also be purified with strong wine. Mother once said that too much wine worsened the injury. The most common use of wine was to drink until one could no longer feel the pain, but Marcus would not allow Bjarn to drink the sour wine in the jar. He could not begin to fathom the purpose of the larvae. Eventually, Marcus decided to start with what he knew. Or at least what he thought he knew.

On a table next to Bjarn stood a washbasin and the water jugs the monk had carried. Marcus poured water into the bowl when he noticed a yellow lump lying on the table. He picked it up, felt it with his fingers and smelled it. A faint scent of lavender. It had to be soap. The Northmen also used soap when washing. The monks and heathens thus had this in common. Marcus washed his face and hands. Small clots of clotted blood dissolved and coloured the water pink. Was he injured? He felt with his fingers but could not find any wounds. Maybe it was not his blood? The thought made him scrub harder.

Finally satisfied with the cleaning, he examined Bjarn and found no other injuries than what was under the brown-stained bandage. He did not understand why the Northman was tied up, as he was obviously unable to escape or injure anyone. On the other hand, he would be able to hurt himself if he tore off his bandages or fell off the table. Marcus decided it was just as well that Bjarn lay still, so he made no attempt to loosen the straps.

Marcus attended to cleaning the wound. With the knife, he cut the bandage covering Bjarn's chest. Then, he pulled the cloth over the wound until he felt the resistance from the linen stuck in dried blood and pus. He continued to pull in a steady motion.

Bjarn awoke and shouted in pain. His head pressed against the band over his forehead, and the muscles in his arms tightened against the straps that were fastened under the table. He glared at Marcus, who calmly continued pulling loose the bandage.

Marcus could not understand what the warrior was saying but recognised some words he had heard in other contexts. He dropped the stained piece of cloth on the floor and smiled.

'Good morning, Bjarn!'

Bjarn's expression changed several times in short order, as the reactions went from pain to surprise to recognition. When he tried to get up, his movements were once again prevented by the straps. He looked upwards towards his forehead with a frustrated grimace.

Marcus reasoned that Bjarn's head could not cause any harm as long as his body was restrained. He leaned forward to loosen the leather band but stopped and held up his palm as a sign that Bjarn should wait. From the shelf, he picked up the silver bowl and started pouring water on the wound with an even, thin stream.

Bjarn recoiled in pain. With clenched teeth, he pushed his head back. His forearms were shaking, but he held his breath and said nothing. Marcus stopped and looked at the result. Blood and water ran down both sides of the table, but there was still too much clotted blood around the wound for him to get a proper look. He put the silver bowl back and fetched the wine and some cloth. After soaking the piece of cloth with wine, he washed away the clots around the wound. Some wine found its way into the wound, and this time Bjarn could not help screaming. Marcus continued to clean the wound while the Northman screamed without words.

After a while, Marcus was satisfied and could see the wound clearly. It lay just below the thin bone that sits between the chest and the shoulder. His father had called it the *clavicula* because that was what it was called in Latin. Marcus and Julia had competed over who knew the Latin names of the most bones, but Marcus could not see how that would help him now. It would have been better if they had learned how to treat wounds.

The wound was wide, but not deeper than the length of a finger, as if it was caused by an arrow with a broad tip. Marcus recalled the arrowheads Ulv had pilfered on the Orkney Islands. They were long and narrow, made to penetrate thick hide or armour. The broad arrowheads of the Irish would do more harm to animals or people with little protection. Bjarn's thick weapon shirt had prevented the arrow from penetrating deep into his chest. It had probably saved him, at least for a while.

After rinsing the wound with water several times, Marcus examined it further. The skin around the wound was red, and there could be more pus deeper down. Marcus considered pulling the edges aside to better clean the wound but feared it would make it heal more slowly. He collected the blood-stained rags and the used bandages and dropped them in front of the door. Then, he washed his hands again and walked over to the window to think.

Marcus still had no idea how to use the herbs or honey, and definitely not the larvae. He could not experiment with treatment he knew nothing about when a mistake could kill

Bjarn. All he knew was what his mother had taught him. Wounds must be kept clean, and he did not come to terms with the thought that there could still be pus deeper in the wound.

He returned to the table. Bjarn had fallen asleep. There was some bleeding from the wound, and a thin streak of blood ran down the left side of his chest. Marcus poured some of the water from the silver bowl into the wine jar, diluting the wine. Then, he pulled the edges of the wound aside and emptied the liquid into the wound. Bjarn awoke once more, roaring with pain. This time, Marcus discerned several crude words that were probably intended as unfavourable descriptions of himself. So be it. He poured wine on a clean piece of cloth, hung it over his little finger and pressed it into the wound to dig out the pus that had accumulated there. Bjarn threw himself from side to side, within the limited range of motion he had. In the stream of words that were shouted at him, Marcus caught a promise of a painful death. Marcus rinsed the wound once more. The Northman calmed down while tears dripped down on the table.

Satisfied with the cleansing of the wound, Marcus decided to cover it with a layer of honey. He had a nagging suspicion that the reason he preferred honey was that he was hungry. Folding a piece of cloth until it was as wide as his palm, he put it on top of the wound. He did not find any suitable clothing to wrap around the chest to fasten it, so he smeared animal fat along the edge of the piece of cloth to make it stick to the skin. After washing the remains of blood and animal grease from his hands, he lay down on his bed.

Bjarn was awake but showed no interest in talking to his tormentor.

CHAPTER 4: VENGEANCE

Browntooth sat to the left of the campfire. Ulv stalked in an arc to the right, bringing him within thirty steps of his prey. The men spoke, but Ulv could not understand a word. He crouched behind a bush and waited. Browntooth waved his arms and showed his rotten teeth, apparently recounting a story he found very entertaining. The memories bubbled up in Ulv. He stalked forward with one arrow on the string and the other three in the hand holding the bow. Aiming at the centre of Browntooth's chest, he advanced slowly. The bow creaked as he pulled the string. A pleasant sound. Anger gave him extra strength, and Ulv drew the string another inch. The good arrow. It was going to hit the vicious man with the ugly teeth, and it was going to hit him hard. Ulv reached the cart. Soon, he would pass within the circle of flickering light. There was no going back. His strength had to hold.

Browntooth's eyes found Ulv when he was less than ten paces away. His mouth gaped and his eyes opened wide. The hands, that were gesticulating to bring the story to life, fell down by his side. Sweat dripped from his forehead. One moment, but it was one of the clearest in Ulv's life. The moment he took revenge. Browntooth's face changed. The cue Ulv was waiting for. He had to make sure the villain knew who was in front of him. Browntooth would know who killed him. And he would know he made a fatal mistake in tying Ulv to a tree.

Ulv exhaled and let his arrow fly.

The arrow drilled into Browntooth's stomach just below the chest. Slightly lower than intended, but a hit that would lead to a painful death. If not a swift one. Browntooth let out a long, low moan.

Browntooth's minions sprang into motion, but Ulv was faster. The second arrow was notched and aimed at the closest of the brigands.

'I have no desire to kill any of you. Browntooth was a vile excuse of a man. I suspect you're just cowards who followed him because you did not dare do anything else. You may live.'

Ulv realised that he was speaking in a language the ruffians were unlikely to understand. He had to keep it simple. He let his aim shift between the three men as he glanced around for his belongings.

A thought struck him like lightning in the tallest tree: *The fifth man!* He had forgotten the last man. Ulv forced himself to be calm while his eyes searched for the unseen enemy.

The man in front of him shifted his weight from one foot to the other. The gaze of one of the others flickered. A slight rustle behind him.

Ulv turned. Not a moment too soon.

The fifth brigand came towards him with an axe raised. Ulv swung the bow towards the man and released the arrow. The man stopped. The arrow protruded from his chest as he took an unsteady step backwards before falling over.

Ulv had forgotten the fifth man. A reminder that he had to be careful, and quick.

He spun around again, with arrow number three nocked. One of the bad ones. He hoped nobody would spare it a closer look. The three men had come closer with weapons drawn. But not close enough.

'Away!' shouted Ulv, once more aiming the arrow back and forth between them.

The men looked at each other. Ulv pulled the bowstring further and aimed at the nearest man. For several breaths, they stood still and glared at each other. Then, the man took a step back and dropped his knife to the ground. Ulv shifted his aim to the next man.

The two remaining men also dropped their weapons. Using simple words and pointing with a bow and arrow, Ulv got one of them to collect his equipment and put it in a sack. Ulv looked around at the barrels and crates scattered in the messy camp. The tent was dirty, torn and patched.

The dark area was not a cave but a boulder with a sloping wall that served as roof over a small space. Underneath lay a dog, whimpering with its head on the ground. Sad eyes looked at Ulv. He pointed his arrow at the man who had finished packing his equipment and made him put the sack down at the edge of the camp. Ulv would like to have retrieved the two used arrows as well, but his strength was fading, and he did not risk spending more time in the company of three enemies. With the arrow aimed at the men, Ulv backed in the direction of his equipment.

'If I see any of you again, you are dead,' Ulv said, standing with the sack by his feet. He took the time to look the three men in the eye, one by one, with what he hoped was a threatening look. Then, he lowered the bow, held it and the arrows in the same hand, threw the sack over his shoulder and slipped in between the trees.

CHAPTER 5: PURPLE

It was a purple day.

Geir Galne was not in his best of moods. He should not complain, the last few days had gone tolerably well. He had not lost any more warriors since Tryggr, or 'Magnus Trygg', as he now called himself, had to prove that he was top dog on the ship many sunrises ago. It ended with Trygg killing two of Geir's men. The two berserks had challenged the veteran and lost. One last, fatal lesson.

It had been a relief to find Vass here in Dyflin. There was something about that Dane. He was closer to Odin than most. On the other hand, Sigurd Jarl was gone. He probably sat with his brothers in Odin's hall and drank mead from Heidrun and ate the meat of the hog Særimne.

Geir sat on a bench outside the round, small house he had taken as his own in the village by the black pool, or *dubh linn* in the tongue of the natives. He slipped on his shoes and took a deep breath. It smelled of sea, waste and mud. Geir closed his eyes. Rotten apple and old cabbage were the most noticeable odours. It was good to get that out of the world. One less thing to contemplate. Thoughts churning on the question that had taken up most of his quiet time in recent days. The way forward.

With Sigurd Jarl dead, Geir was free to take his berserks and move on. In reality, they were all *wolfskins*, but it seemed that people nowadays were too lazy to call things by their real names. Thus, they were called berserks, even though none of them wore bear pelts. Maybe he should start calling the other warriors farmers? No, that was too apt. Cows, perhaps? No, it was too obvious. But he could begin mooing at them. After all, he had a reputation to maintain. Geir shook his head. He found a straw, broke it to the right length and put it in the corner of his mouth.

It was a day to make a decision. He should use his quiet time for that, not to ponder names. Nor was it a day to look behind, but a day to choose the path forward. A purple day. The morning sun warmed his face. Some chickens clucked. An axe chopped at timber. No, two axes, two logs. Steps. Somebody approached. There was a slight chance that this somebody would pass by. A man could certainly hope. The steps came closer. Sobbing footsteps in the mud. Boots? One of Torgils's men? The footsteps stopped. Maybe three feet away. The man inhaled. As if he was afraid to disturb. Geir did not allow the man to speak first.

'I'm going to talk to him.'

'What?' the man replied after a long moment of silence.

Geir opened one eye to look at the uninvited visitor. Had he been wrong? No, it was one of Torgils's men. In a heavy weapon shirt and high leather boots. Just slow, then. As expected. Dim wit spread rapidly around here. Geir closed his eyes again. How could anyone think that slow? Geir envisioned a water-powered wheel similar to what the Irish used in their mills. A wheel that barely moved, driven by a small river or a brook. That was how it must be in this man's head. In most men's heads. Geir never had problems with his wheel going too slow. His wheel was driven by a rushing river. Occasionally a waterfall. The problem was that there were many wheels in his head, and they were not driven by the same stream. Sometimes, the wheel connected to his speech might be slow, while his thought-wheel could be driven by a waterfall. Or the wheel that bound to his hearing could tell him that one of the six hens was dissatisfied with something. *Cluck, cluck, CLUCK-CLUCK.* Clearly unhappy with something.

The visitor said something.

'I'm going to talk to Vass. Go and bark up another tree,' said Geir.

The man remained still. At seven, Geir thought. *One, two, three, four, five, six.* The man turned and left. Six. Not bad. This man knew how to make an impression! Quicker in the head than a medium whetstone. His name was Svein. Or was it Stein? Stein fitted best. Stein from now on.

Geir moved the straw to the other corner of his mouth. A purple day. The way forward. He had to get south if he was to have any chance of finding her. There was talk that Ragnar and the Danes would travel before winter. At the same time, there was something in him that said that the time was not right to travel yet. The Danes were no worse than others. They stank, but most did. Not as much as the Irish, in any case. They were not in the habit of washing. Unless they stumbled in the mud after too much beer. *Laugar-day* was just an ordinary, smelly day for these savages. No wonder the Irish women favoured the newcomers. Washing once a week was unheard of among the Irish. Combs were not in custom, either. It was unfathomable there were still people on this island.

Geir took a deep breath. To his inner eye, he picked up a knife and threw it into the future. He followed the blade. Somewhere along that path, he would travel south. To Seville, perhaps? Or even further. There, he would find her. But when? It was too late in the fall to get far.

Nevertheless, there was time to return to Horthaland before winter. Or perhaps to Hedeby. From there, ships often sailed south. He could take his berserks there. They could be in Seville early next spring. He could ask Ragnar where the Danes were sailing.

Or he could stay in Dyflin and see what happened over the winter. There would be a dogfight with the Irish sooner or later. By no means safe. The alternative – long days with little to do and too much quiet time – was just as bad. Something needed to happen. Then, there would be only one river and one wheel. With nothing else to focus his mind, he could eat mushrooms. That made others wild and bloodthirsty, but he became clear as still water. Mushrooms slowed most of his rivers and wheels. With only one wheel spinning at a time, he could assume the role of Galne. Through a long and tedious winter, however, he could rely on calming his mind on mushrooms. He had seen what happened to those who ate too often.

Geir Galne got up. There was help for those who sought it. Aud could look into the future. It was not every day he wanted to know something about his own destiny, but today was not every day.

Today was a purple day.

*

Aud stared at the rune stones scattered over the linen cloth. It smelled of dried flowers and fresh herbs. And something else. Something foul-smelling that made Geir uneasy. As if something was kept out of sight.

'I see a man. A small man.' Aud turned a couple of the stones as if to read them better. 'He's searching too. You have to help him to help yourself.'

Geir opened his mouth to ask who the little man was and who he was looking for. What he needed help with. But he did not utter the words. It did not seem like a good idea to disturb the volve as she read the future.

'I see more. A big bear. A little wolf. And the god of war. They are all a part of the whole,' Aud continued.

Geir shifted his gaze from the rune stones to Aud while he waited for the continuation. *Loke's balls, she had to give him something more?! A big bear and a little wolf. Should he go searching in the woods? This was just …*

He stopped the stream of thought. His gaze moved from the volve to the rune stones once more. He forced himself to relax and pull a neutral expression across his face.

'That's what I see.' Aud picked up the stones again. 'As for your second question ...' The rune stones clinked between her delicate hands. Like the teeth of a frozen man. Before the stones again rolled across the canvas. Like the teeth of a rude man. Like the teeth of the man who had first given him the nickname Galne. *The mad.* Apparently, one was not supposed to slap a man across the face for such impudence. Not with the blunt end of the axe, anyway. With both hands on the shaft. While the man had his head back, laughing, with his mouth open.

And, of course, that did not make the name less fitting.

The man had eaten nothing but soup and porridge after that.

'Hmm ...,' said Aud, low and hoarse.

It got quiet. Geir shuddered. Regretting that he had asked the second question, he opened his mouth to stop the volve. Too late.

'Safe ... You are safe when you feel insecure. You are in danger when you feel safe.'

'What? Where?' Geir had so many questions that he could not form a single one.

'This is what the gods are showing me tonight. Nobody gets more than they deserve.' Aud looked at him with narrowed eyes. Challenged him. Encouraged him to question the prediction. To challenge the gods. And her. Geir knew better. He often questioned the gods. He was not afraid to challenge them, and he was convinced that they appreciated men who were not afraid to speak their minds. The Norse gods were not like the White Christ, who wanted obedient lambs. But her? He was not stupid enough to question Aud's practice or anything else about her.

'You can go now, Galne,' Aud said.

Geir nodded and got up from the bench. The wheels in his head spun. Quickly.

He needed time for himself.

Quiet time.

CHAPTER 6: BASTARD

Ulv slumped down under a spruce tree with low, dense branches. He knew he should have gone further. Should have hidden his tracks and checked if anyone followed. It was just not possible. His strength ran out and sleep overtook him.

Ulv listened at the door. Impatience tore at him like a storm pulling at a bush. He stared into the crack. There was no point opening the door before the man at the table had turned his back. He sat with needle and thread repairing a cloak. His dark hair was tied together in a ponytail, and his short, dark beard had grey areas below the corners of his mouth. The dark, concentrated eyes glittered under bushy eyebrows. The only light came from the small fireplace in the middle of the room. On the table in front of the man lay the knife. The one that Ulv had to get hold of. Ulv shifted his weight from one foot to the other and stared at the working hands. The rest of the man could not be seen through the narrow opening. Down, in, under, back, up and through. The needle moved across the fabric – steady and sure. It would soon be time to act; he could feel it, his hand slid towards the handle. It had to be time. The needle came down towards the fabric again, but this time it did not go through. It slid down along the cloth and under the last stitch. The hands lowered the piece of cloth towards the table.

Ulv gripped the handle. He could see the man's head as he got up. The man disappeared from sight for a moment, then he reappeared. He moved towards the hearth. Would he put another log on the fire? Ulv put his ear to the crack. Soon he heard a scratching sound of wood against stone. Ulv envisioned the man as he stoked the fire. He would turn around to pick up a couple of logs. It went quiet. Ulv pushed the handle, slipped in, closed the door and squeezed down between the bench and the wall to his right. From there, he would crawl along the wall by the bench until he got behind where the man had sat. Then he would cross over to the other side and come back at the opposite side of the table, which stood in the middle of the room. He had to bring the string he had fastened at the bottom of the door with him all the way.

The man turned back towards the hearth and placed a log on the fire. Careful and accurate, as if it were the last stone in a wall. As if it only would fit in this one place. Then he put the other log in place with the same precision. He leaned down and blew, and Ulv could hear the crackle from the wood as flames flared up. Crawling along the bench, Ulv stopped at the end and looked at the man from behind the bench leg. The man stood with his palms outstretched against the flames, staring at the dancing pillars of red and yellow light. Ulv did not look directly at the fire. He stayed under the bench and waited.

The man rubbed his hands and went back to the table. He sat down and went back to work. The man sat with his side towards Ulv, and Ulv could see the wrinkles on his forehead as the man focused on his sewing. Ulv was confident he could move behind and around the man without being seen. The man had just stared into the flames, and Ulv crouched in the darkest part of the room. Checking that the string had not snagged on anything, he began to crawl further along the wall coming behind the man's back. From the corner of the room, he followed the wall and crossed to the other side. From there, he would crawl up by the man's right side. He wrapped the thread around a bucket of water and continued. Pressing himself towards the floor, he crawled – fingerbreadth after fingerbreadth. The going was slow, unimaginably slow, but he knew he had to be as close to the ground as possible for the last part.

He came to another bench. Crawling under the seat, he continued under the table. Now he was as close to the knife as he could get. Unfortunately, that meant he was also very, very close to the man. The man hummed a tune. The words were not discernible, but it sounded like the song about Tor and Siv. Ulv sat halfway up under the table, just below where the knife lay. He looked down at the thread he was holding in his left hand. It went along the floor past the man, along the left part of the water bucket, from there it was no longer visible, but he hoped it still went halfway around the bucket, over the floor and to the bench where he first hid, around the leg and back towards the door. His heart pounded in his throat. This was the tricky part. The dangerous part. He looked towards the door and began to pull the string.

Nothing happened. Ulv followed the string with his eyes. It lay along the floor to the bucket. Maybe if he could lift the cord a little? It must not get stuck under. He made a quick motion with his hand, and the string waved away. It rose a little from the ground, and Ulv gently pulled back. Nothing happened yet. He pulled harder, stared at the door, and worried that something else would give way and move. His patience was as thin and uncertain as the first autumn ice. Then he felt it. Something gave way. Big, round eyes stared at the door. It moved. Time to go for it.

The cord tightened around the bucket, around the bench leg, and around the outer plank of the door. The door slid open, and a gust of cold air rushed across the floor like an invisible wave. The little boy's hand shot up over the edge of the table to where the knife lay. It bumped into something. Something tumbled over the tabletop. Ulv pulled his hand back. A bang sounded, and his hand stopped. Ulv looked over the edge of the table and saw his shirt sleeve pinned to the table by the knife. A mug lay on its side, and water dripped on to the floor. The man continued humming and looked down at his hands as he worked.

The needle came up through the piece of cloth, down, through and up again.

The man put cloth, needle and thread on the table, got up and walked around the table. There he loosened the string in the plank, closed the door and wound the string around his right hand as he walked back towards the table. The little boy detached the knife from the table and his sleeve and wiped his eyes with the same sleeve. New tears flooded his eyes. Not because he was in pain. Or because the noise or the knife had scared him. Nor because he was afraid of the man. The tears came because he had lost. He was hopeless. A little bastard, as Bjørn used to say.

The man sat down. 'The string was a good idea, Ulv.'

'When did you discover me?' Ulv asked in a thin voice, almost a whisper.

'Not until you were under the table here. Did you get impatient when you could not get the door open?'

'No!'

'Perhaps you should have waited until I got up again, by myself?'

'You said the cord was a good idea!'

'Yes, it was. And if you were in a hurry, then it would be the right choice as well. Were you in a hurry, Ulv?'

'Yes!' replied Ulv with defiance in his voice.

The man smiled. 'But how were you going to get out?'

Ulv's eyes narrowed. 'That was not part of the task!'

'No, you're right,' the man laughed. 'You did good, Ulv. Really good. You hid well in the shadows. Next time, I think you will make it.'

Ulv could not help but smile. Like when a wolf pup tries to look angry and dangerous but is too happy and playful to quite make it.

'Move closer to the fire, and I'll get you some porridge. Bedtime soon,' the man continued.

'I'm not tired, Father!' Ulv said and yawned.

Ulv startled. Something was moving in the bushes nearby. It was morning. He could not see anyone. Something rustled, then it became quiet before it rustled once more. As if somebody was trying to be quiet and sneak upon him. Ulv reached for the seax. It was probably the men from the camp who had tracked him down. If they were that close, they would find him, but there was nothing he could do. He could just hope they would not see him under the tree. A branch snapped behind him, and he turned. More noises. The men from the camp. It had to be them. He stared back where he had heard the last sound.

A leg appeared.

CHAPTER 7: ABBOT

The first light of day signalled the end of a long October night, and Marcus had barely closed his eyes. Bjarn had seemed so troubled that Marcus loosened the straps and let the Northman sleep in his bed. It seemed like an unnecessary burden to let him lie on the wooden table. His suspicions were confirmed when he lay on the table and tried in vain to get some sleep.

Before Marcus got close to dozing off, Bjarn's wound started bleeding because of his constant twisting and turning. Marcus spent the darkest hours of the night moving the dazed, but strong and reluctant, Northman back to the table. When he had fastened the straps, tended the wound and changed the bandages, the night was over.

Marcus did not stir when somebody removed the bar outside the door. Instead, he pretended to be sleeping and lay motionless on his back with his eyes closed and his arms crossed over his chest. Hopefully, the intruder would leave if he faked sleep. The water splashed in his face washed away all hopes of sleep or rest.

Marcus sprang to his feet and wiped water from his eyes. An old man in a brown monk's robe was facing him, with the look and demeanour of a man of authority. He had dark grey eyebrows, a moustache, and a white beard that formed a small point under his chin. His short white hair was shaved in a wedge-shaped tonsure.

Marcus recognised the elderly monk as the man who had stood before him as he knelt in the woods waiting to die. He felt he should say *thank you*, but he could not decide which language would be appropriate to address this man. The monk beat him to it.

The expression on his face and the tone of voice indicated that he had asked a short question, but Marcus did not comprehend a word. The monk made another attempt. The strange sounds and the way his lips moved made Marcus think that he might have spoken in a language that was different from the first. The voice was deep and pleasant, but the result was the same. Marcus did not understand a word.

'Quis es?' asked the old man.

Marcus was relieved to finally understand. He answered in Latin, as his father had taught him. 'I am Marcus, son of Gaius, a merchant from Northumbria.'

The monk did not seem prepared for that answer. His expression revealed doubt, and his tone sounded irritable.

'Why are in the company of the heathens who plague our lands, Marcus, son of Gaius?'

'I'm a slave. At least, I was. Now, I do not know what I am.'

He pointed at Bjarn, still sleeping on the table. 'Maybe I'm his slave now. Or yours?' Marcus shrugged and looked back at the old monk.

'You are not a slave. We need to learn what else you might be. You speak Latin with a good vocabulary but with many errors. Where did you learn that?'

'My father knew many languages. He taught me to read, write and speak Latin. I understand the priests' masses and sermons, but I am not used to speaking to others in Latin.'

'Impressive. Are you a Christian, Marcus, son of Gaius?'

'We went to church as often as we could,' Marcus replied, looking down.

The false words tasted bitter as they dripped from his lips. It was difficult to lie in a monastery. To remedy the situation, he added:

'My village, Wucestre, was consecrated to Saint Cuthbert by King Ceolwulf when he relinquished the throne to become a monk at Lindisfarne a hundred years ago.'

'I see,' the monk replied dryly.

Marcus blushed. The monk had probably heard hundreds of lies and half-lies.

'By the way, I'm not your master. I am our Lord's servant on earth. My name is Cearan, and I am the abbot of St. Columba's Abbey in Kells. Tell me how you got here.'

'I was enslaved by Vikings a month ago. My father was killed, and my sister abducted. I believe she's now a slave to a brutal chieftain called Torgils. They brought me to the Orkney Islands, which the Northmen call the Norðreyjar. On our voyage from there to here, the man who owned me disappeared. We rowed up the Blackwater when our ship was attacked by the Irish. I jumped ashore and tried to stay alive. I happened upon the wounded Jarl and stayed with him until he was killed. You already know the rest of the story. Now I am here and do not know if I am a slave or a free man.'

'You have my sympathy for your losses,' Cearan replied. He looked down and mumbled a short prayer.

Marcus seized the opportunity while the otherwise stern monk looked harmless.

'If I'm not your slave or prisoner, I ask your permission to leave this place today. I have to find my sister.'

Cearan frowned.

'How are you going to find her?'

'If she was captured by the Vikings, I think she's with Torgils in Dyflin. If she escaped, she's without food and shelter near Wucestre, unless she has travelled to Woodhorn.'

'Your plan is to go to Dubh Linn, defeat Torgils and his army and find your sister? And if you do not find her there, will you build a boat, row across a sea full of heathen longships and find her in Northumbria before winter sets in?'

Marcus nodded slowly.

Cearan continued. 'Torgils has taken Dubh Linn by the Liffey, and the Jarl called Glumra holds Linn Duachaill by the Glyde, just north of the Boyne. The heathens have fortified their *longphorts* with palisades and have several hundred trained warriors. Torgils and his witch will slay any monk or Christian they get hold of. Or they will do something much worse, as they have done many times before. The King of Meath cannot capture either Linn Duachaill or Dubh Linn, even if he managed to unite the clans. You would not be able to set foot in Torgils's camp, let alone find your sister.'

'I have no choice. I promised to find her.'

'Then you are a brave young man.'

The monk's face was gentle and friendly now. He put an arm around Marcus and led him out of the room.

'Perhaps there is another way. Let me show you around the monastery.'

CHAPTER 8: SMALL

A small man. He would start with that. Find out who the small man was.

Geir sat once more on the bench outside his roundhouse. Who was the smallest man in Dyflin? There was a small man named Stig among Sigurd's men, barely taller than a boy. The smith had been nicknamed Stubbs for a reason. Of course, it did not have to be that simple. Geir did not have much experience with divination or prophecies, but one thing he had learned from the stories of those who had glimpsed into the days yet to come: it was rarely straightforward. Never easy.

Could it be Kjetil? Kjetil Korte. *Korte* meant 'short one'. Maybe that was what the runes meant. Also, Aud had spoken about a giant bear. If Kjetil was not the small man by being Korte, there was always a chance that he was the big bear. He had to talk to Kjetil, but he wanted to start with Stubbs. Geir sighed and got to his feet.

Asking around, he found Stig Stubbs in the northern part of town, where he and some other men were setting up a smithy.

'Stig?' said Geir.

The stocky man turned with a questioning expression on his red face. When he saw who was asking, a furrow appeared on his forehead. Geir did not waste time exchanging meaningless words.

'I can help you find what you're looking for,' Geir continued.

Stig did not seem to be able to answer.

'So, what are you looking for, Stig?' Geir waved his hand impatiently.

'What do you mean, berserk?'

'Wolfskin,' Geir replied, annoyed by people who could not tell the difference between berserks and wolfskins.

'What?' Stig said, wiping sweat from his forehead.

Geir considered leaving. He could not possibly be intended to help this dimwit with anything. But the prophecy was far too important not to be examined from all angles. He sighed and considered how he could make things clear to the short-sighted dwarf.

'Let's say you are a little pig ...'

It may not have been the best choice of words, but they were the words that popped into his head as his gaze fixed on the round, blushing face.

'A piglet, rather, who has gotten away from his mother. Or sow, if you will. Then you would be looking for ...?'

'The sow?' said Stig, confused as a piglet who has lost his mother.

'Exactly! And I could help you. So, what are you looking for?'

'Mum?'

'Are you looking for your mother?'

'No, but you said so, didn't you?'

Geir Galne turned and left.

The gods probably meant short and not small. They must have meant short. Definitely.

Geir found Kjetil Korte outside a house where he was attempting to repair an old bench, without tools. Kjetil looked up at Geir with a grimace that said: 'What does *he* want with me?'

'I can help you find what you are looking for,' said Geir,

trying to be more precise from this time.

Kjetil straightened and stared at Geir. Many would say that Kjetil had one of the slowest thought-wheels. However, Geir knew it was not quite that simple. The man had a big, heavy wheel. So, it would take a while to get it started. When it did start, however, it had good speed. Big man, large wheel. But it was not that straightforward. In Geir's experience, a man's size was no indication of what was inside his head. He waited a while longer so that the giant could get the wheel turning.

'What am I looking for?' said Kjetil.

'Are you looking for anything? Or anyone? Is there anything you are searching for?' Geir tried to be patient.

'The thrall?' Kjetil asked.

Of course. Geir knew who this man wanted to get hold of. Everybody who had not been hiding under a rock in recent weeks knew that.

'Yes. Shall I help you find him?'

To help himself, he had to help the small man find what he was looking for. That was what Aud had said. That was the message from the gods. And even if Kjetil was the giant bear, anyone was better off being on good terms with him.

'Yes, you're welcome to find him. But why? Why do *you* want to find him?' said Kjetil.

Geir had not expected that question. He could reply something incomprehensible, and Flatnose would probably not think twice about it. Still, he did not want this to be an incident people talked about. Better if it was not known to everybody that he was looking for the thrall. A solution that was easier to swallow, like a sip of fresh milk, would be preferable.

'It is quite possible I need a favour from you in the not-so-distant future, Kjetil. So an agreement in that direction would be beneficial.' Geir tried to use clever words and refrain from talking in pictures so as not to confuse the giant in this vital matter. 'An agreement that involves me doing this specific service for you, obtaining the lost thrall and handing him over to you. And in return, you provide a service of similar value for me. Deal?'

The big man opened his mouth as if to say something, but no sound came forth. Geir saw the confusion in the man's eyes and decided to push on instead of explaining things again. With the conversation with Stig Stubbs fresh in his mind, it did not seem that explaining things twice was a good alternative.

'Deal?' Geir repeated.

'Yes, fair enough, deal,' replied the giant, scratching his chin with a large fist.

'Marvellous!' Geir said, before he turned and left.

It was taken care of. He would help Kjetil Korte find the thrall and thus help himself. He had no idea *how* this would help, but that was not important. He would leave those details to the gods.

Now, all he had to do was to get the barrel rolling.

CHAPTER 9: INVENTORY

The deer lifted its head. Its brown ear turned this way and that. Its nostril widened. Then it trotted off. Moving slowly, but still at great speed. A calf followed in its mother's footsteps. Not as graceful, but with childish zeal on long legs.

Ulv closed his eyes once more. He had to move on. Find a good campsite. Water and food. He was parched and famished.

Soon.

Ulv sat on the floor with his back against the wall in Sigurd Jarl's Hall and listened to Father telling a story about Odin. More precisely, the tale of when Odin went to Mime in Jotunheimen to drink from the well of wisdom. It was a well-known tale and not the most exciting one. The words became a hum in the background while Ulv looked around the room. The Jarl sat in the high seat at the centre of the table. In front of him stood a horn with beer. His hands clasped around it as if it was his dearest possession. It was large and had silver fittings. He had pushed away a tray with a half-eaten shank of lamb. Ulv's stomach rumbled. They did not always remember that he needed food. Next to the Jarl sat an old warrior. The man looked funny. His lower teeth protruded in front of his upper teeth, and he was bald except for a few tufts of white hair around his ears. Something reminiscent of the hairs on the ears of a lynx he and Father had seen that spring. The old man prodded the Jarl with his elbow, leaned closer and said something while his gaze followed a young thrall girl who passed by on the other side of the table with an empty jug in her hands. Ulv glanced at the girl. She was darker in complexion and had black hair. Around sixteen winters old, she could probably be considered a woman. With quick and steady steps, she danced away from sluggish hands grabbing at her.

'In return, I'll give you my left eye.' Father's voice, in a part of the story that Ulv enjoyed. 'I have come far and will not leave with this matter unresolved,' continued Father, who recounted how Odin came to sacrifice his eye for wisdom.

Ulv noticed that somebody was staring at him and shifted his gaze back to the Jarl. However, it was not him, but the man standing just behind. The Jarl's closest thrall. His gaze was intense. Ulv got the feeling that the man could see more than usual. As if he could study your mind and see your soul. His eyes were not unfriendly but fierce. Otherwise, the man seemed ordinary. Brown hair, a crooked nose and a beardless face. Simple but clean clothes. Ulv looked away. The end of the story was approaching. The men in the hall were getting drunk, and it was time to quit. Father had explained that when men had drunk too much beer, they lost interest in everything except women and fighting. At that point, it did not matter how good the story was or how vividly it was told.

Ulv met Father's eyes and realised it was time. Father always sent him out when the men had been drinking too much and for too long. If it was not too cold. Slipping out the door at the end of the longhouse, he sat down on a rock by the bathhouse. He took out the little Tor's hammer Father had whittled and practised one of the tricks Father had taught him. With deft movements, he made the hammer disappear up his sleeve again and again. The door to the longhouse opened, and a man came out. It was the thrall with the intense eyes. He glanced around before he started towards Ulv. In his hands, he had a bowl of food. Closing the distance, he held out the dish.

'Hungry? I brought some soup with meat and bread for you.' The thrall smiled, but the smile did not reach his eyes. The voice, on the other hand, was friendly, and the food smelled delicious.

'Thank you.' Accepting the food, Ulv shifted on the stone and asked if the man would sit. The slave raised his eyebrows for a moment before sitting down. It went quiet except for the sound of Ulv slurping mouthfuls of soup.

'Good?' The man broke the silence.

Ulv glanced up at the man next to him. The young thrall smiled, and it struck Ulv that he might be hungry too.

'Do you want some?' Ulv held out the bowl. The man looked at the food, then at Ulv, but made no movement to take it. Maybe he did not want to eat the soup that Ulv had already eaten from? Ulv put the bowl on his lap, took the piece of bread and broke it in two. He handed the largest chunk to the man. The young man accepted the bread.

'Haven't you learned how to treat slaves?'

'Father says I should treat every man with respect.'

'Then your father is a better man than I.'

Ulv looked at the man as he swallowed a piece of bread. He wondered what the thrall meant. The question must have been evident on his face, for the man replied:

'I would only show respect to those who deserve it. And those I have to show respect because of their position in the world. And that's most people since I'm a slave.' He smiled resignedly and shrugged. 'But you, young man, you deserve my respect,' he continued, nodding at Ulv. 'I must get back to serve men I have less respect for. Thanks for the bread ...' The man finished in a tone that made it sound like a question.

'Ulv.'

'Around here I am called Emil,' said the man and went back into the longhouse.

*

The next day Ulv and Father made their way home

from Sigurd Jarl's farm. Father had traded some new tools and arrowheads for the four fox furs and two hare furs they had carried with them. They had no horse, so they had to carry everything. It was heavy, but the weather was good, and they were not in a hurry.

'What did you learn yesterday?' Father asked without taking his eyes off the path winding its way over the hill some distance in front of them. Ulv did not like such questions. He never understood what Father was looking for. He did not answer. Father squinted down at him. 'What can you tell me about old Erling?'

'He was old, crooked and hairless, except for the long white tufts around his ears,' replied Ulv. Of all the games he and Father played when they had a free moment, this was the one he liked the least. Father never seemed satisfied with his answers. Not that he expressed dissatisfaction or disappointment, but there was rarely any praise to be had either. Thus, he went for a defiant reply he knew Father would not be impressed by.

'So what you're saying is that yesterday you learned that old Erling is old?'

'Yes, exactly.'

'We have a long way to go, Ulv.'

'What do you want to know, then?'

'I heard that Sigurd Jarl was worried about old Erling, and he whispered to one of the men that he was afraid that the old man was tired of life and would throw himself off the cliff by the edge of the forest. Erling overheard it and was furious with the Jarl for talking so demeaning about him.'

Father kept his face straight forward, but Ulv could feel the sidelong glance.

'I don't believe that.'

'What?'

'Your story,' Ulv said, thinking of what he had seen and

heard inside the longhouse. Several things did not fit with Father's story, but he could not quite pinpoint them. He needed more time to put the parts together.

'I understood,' replied Father, 'but what was wrong with my story?'

'We have passed the forest edge twice in two days. There is no cliff there.'

'It may be that it is hidden or that they spoke of another forest edge. What else?'

'That old man would not have been able to hear any whispers.'

'Oh?'

'Yes, he is hard of hearing,' Ulv replied, unable to keep the triumph out from his voice.

'Why do you say that?'

'All old men have hearing problems.'

'What?'

'All old men have hearing problems,' said Ulv, louder.

'What?' Father replied in a raised voice.

'All old ...' then Ulv finally understood what his father was doing and went quiet. Father laughed. Ulv remained silent. He did not like to be made fun of. Even less than stupid games.

When they came to a large tree, Father picked up the conversation again.

'Was that all? Was that all you learned?'

Ulv sighed before answering. 'When Erling leaned over to talk to the Jarl, he spoke too loudly. It seemed like he was going to whisper, but he almost shouted. That's why I think he is hard of hearing.' It was quiet for a moment. 'Besides,' continued Ulv, 'he joked with the Jarl and stared at the young thrall girl like a hungry man drooling at a roast pig.'

Father gave him another sidelong glance but said

nothing.

'So I do not think he's tired of living or is going to jump off a cliff any time soon,' Ulv said before it went quiet once more.

'Anything else then?'

'No,' replied Ulv before continuing on an impulse. 'Yes, you're starting to lose your grip as a storyteller.'

'Oh?'

'Yes, the men drank too much beer. You had to quit early. You should have chosen a more cheerful story.'

'You may be right, Ulv, you may be right. But perhaps the mood was bad for stories in the first place?'

When Ulv did not answer, Father continued. 'How was the Jarl's mood?'

Ulv thought. He wanted to answer 'bad' because it suited his own mood there and then. Besides, he felt it was accurate, but he did not quite know why, so he remained silent.

Instead, Father continued. 'Did you notice how little the Jarl ate?' It's unusual for a man of his size. And how he clutched his drinking horn with both hands. How he did not joke and laugh?'

Ulv nodded thoughtfully.

'Something bothered the Jarl, but I do not know exactly what. Maybe that he has no heir or that the farm does not produce enough? Maybe something completely different, I do not know. But something bothered him, that's for sure.' Father stared at the horizon.

They had entered the woods when Father spoke once more, with exaggerated elation, as if to shake off less pleasant thoughts. 'Let me give you a question I think you would like better: Who was the most dangerous man in there?'

'The thrall,' replied Ulv, without a second thought.

'The thrall? The Jarl's house thrall? The one who stood right behind where the Jarl sat? Why him?'

'His eyes.'

The sun was high in the sky when Ulv opened his eyes again. It took him a while to figure out where he was and why he was there. Supporting his weight against a tree trunk, he got to his feet. For a time, he just stood there, gathering his thoughts and listening. His fear that the men from the camp were still looking for him was still present. The forest around him made only the usual noises as he tried to orient himself. It had to be about noon, and hence, the sun would be straight south. He had gone west to get to the brigand's camp. Southwest seemed like a sensible direction. He took a deep breath and set off.

Not long after, he realised that he had a sack over his shoulder, with all the equipment he had gotten away with. He had to chuckle when he also noticed that he was wandering around almost naked. Needing no more pretext to rest, he slumped to the ground. Sitting in the heather with his back to a large tuft, he opened the sack. He pulled out the tunic, the cloak, the wool trousers, the belt bag, the water skin, the leather shoes and the seax with sheath and belt. Flint, steel and the scarf were still in the belt bag. Also, the pieces of dry, flat bread from the day he left Dyflin lay there. Three days ago? He was not sure anymore, and it did not matter. He picked up the pieces of bread and munched on them. It was even drier now, but it was the best he had eaten since the blot on the Norðreyjar. The water skin contained a few mouthfuls of water, and he rinsed down the bread with the last drops. He soon felt better. As if he were a human being. He removed the threads, leaves and remnants of moss he had tied around his upper body.

The cut across his chest was covered with clotted blood. Otherwise, it did not look too bad, but he would not know for sure until he could clean it. He pulled on his wool trousers, tunic and shoes. Tightened his belt with the belt pouch and seax. Holding the bow and the two crooked arrows in his hand, he got up and started off towards the southwest.

Fresh water and a safe campsite were his next goals.

CHAPTER 10: LINN DUACHAILL

Kjetil Korte's ship was the first to arrive at Linn Duachaill on a chilly morning in late October, followed by Torgils's and Ragnar's longships. Vass made sure to be too late to rejoin his crewmates under Kjetil Korte's command as they departed from Dyflin the day before. After witnessing the brutal, flat-nosed Jarl's treatment of Ulv, he had stayed away whenever possible.

Neither was he tempted to travel with Torgils and Aud. The volve was one of the few people Vass was afraid of. There were no limits to her cruel imagination, nor to her absolute conviction she was carrying out the will of the gods. Instead, Vass had jumped aboard Ragnar's ship at the last moment. The Dane chieftain had nodded as if he understood. Vass liked the old man, who had won many battles and killed more enemies than anyone else. Still, there was a calmness over him that made others feel safe.

Øystein Glumra's fortified longphort was built in the same way as Dyflin, only smaller. Three ships lay with their bows in the air and formed the roofs of large longhouses. Four others were pulled up on the beach. One last longship was supported on beams. The mast was broken, and the hull was damaged in several places. Vass shuddered at the sight of Magnus Trygg's damaged ship, on which he had been on board when they sailed from Sandøy.

Kjetil, Torgils, Aud and Ragnar were received by Øystein Mørejarl and his hird. The crew quickly spread around the camp, in search of friends, beer or women. Vass did not know whom he was hoping to find. He had already met Geir Galne and did not desire to spend more time with him. Many good men had fallen in battle with the Irish, and Ulv was as outlawed here as in Dyflin.

Vass stopped at an open space above the beach. A young boy, no more than twelve winters, sparred with a wooden sword. The youngster was agile and quick. The muscular legs and how he handled the heavy shield proved that the boy possessed strength beyond his years. Vass smiled. He recognised attack patterns and movements he had practised at the same age. The boy would develop into a deadly warrior if he lived long enough.

But it was his opponent who caught Vass's attention. He had seen women wielding weapons before, but never like this. The helmet and padded shirt covered her face and body, but the way she moved revealed that this was no man.

With her spear, she knocked the boy's wooden sword aside again and again. When he got too eager, he got a rap on the shoulder, knee or elbow with the blunt end of the weapon. Still, she was gentle and avoided humiliating her inferior opponent – until the very end.

The boy swung forcefully at the woman's right side. The spear guided his sword harmlessly past her hip, causing him to lose his balance. The fair-haired woman spun around once, put her foot against his buttocks and sent him face down to the ground. He lay on his stomach until the laughter from the spectators had subsided. The woman removed her helmet and helped him to his feet.

Vass confirmed what he already knew: the shieldmaiden was gorgeous. She radiated an irresistible strength and confidence. When their eyes met, it was the berserk who looked down. He adjusted his belt and rubbed his face to hide the blush he knew would be visible to the whole world. When he looked up, the woman had put her arm around the young boy's shoulder, and together they walked away from the makeshift arena.

'Sigrid and Ragnvald, Øystein Mørejarl's children,' sounded a familiar voice behind him.

Vass turned and looked into Magnus Trygg's smiling face.

'Trygg!' he exclaimed, throwing his arms around the old warrior in a bear hug.

After a moment, they began thumping each other's backs with their fists.

'I'm pleased to see you, too, Vass!' Trygg replied when he had freed himself.

'I thought you fell by the Blackwater!'

'Close enough. Many others did. But Odin has no use for old men like me.'

'You have to tell me what happened.'

'I will, but I need to talk to Torgils first. Wash, and find a girl to hug. You will find me in the mead hall in a while.'

Vass nodded and followed the instructions.

*

The large hall was packed with Northmen and Danes. Vass stood taller than most and worked his way through the crowd. He found his target, grabbed his shoulder and pulled him around, so he spilt beer over them both.

'Arngrim!' Vass shouted in greeting before the man had regained his balance.

'Vass?' replied the Northman with equal amounts of irritation, joy and surprise. 'I thought you stayed behind at Hoy!'

Arngrim had been among those of Magnus Trygg's men Vass liked best. His tongue was sharp, but he was friendly and reliable.

'No. We climbed to the top and down again and continued the journey on Ragnar's ship. That's why we disembarked at Dyflin instead of rowing up the Blackwater with you.' Vass looked around the hall. 'I think your story is longer than mine. Let's find a table so I can hear it.'

Despite there being too few benches to accommodate the number of thirsty patrons in the crowded hall, the pair soon found vacant seats. They exchanged worried glances when they realised the cause but shrugged and sat down next to the man who had been occupying a table all alone until then.

Geir Galne stared intensely into his mead horn and greeted them with a deep and drawn-out belch. His bulging eyes were even redder than usual.

'Good day to you, too!' Vass greeted him with a smile.

Galne appeared to have started drinking to Sigurd Jarl's honour earlier than most. Probably a couple of days before. He looked like a man who had fallen asleep in manure after a feast and smelled even worse.

Geir Galne emptied the horn in response and pounded it on the table but said nothing.

Vass and Arngrim had given up conversing with him when Galne suddenly shouted something incomprehensible and got up from the bench. He staggered out the door, leaving behind a broad trail of angry men.

'Nice man,' Arngrim said.

'He's not that bad,' Vass replied.

'Who is worse?' Arngrim asked.

Unable to come up with many candidates, Vass changed the subject:

'What happened to you?'

Arngrim sighed and drank from his own horn.

'The Irish were waiting for us at the Blackwater. They felled trees over our ships and launched a barrage of arrows at us. We jumped ashore to take up the fight, but they withdrew, away from the river. Our men were scattered, and the Jarl and his hird ran into the main force of the Irish. More than a hundred men strong. The Jarl fell, and many with him.'

Arngrim emptied his horn in silence. With an apologetic expression, he left the table and later returned with two full horns of beer. Vass got one.

Behind him followed Geir Galne, also with two horns. He kept both for himself.

Arngrim nodded at Galne as he resumed the story.

'Galne took the Jarl's ship. Trygg's ship was damaged and had drifted some distance down the river. A tree that had been felled over the ship was stuck in the bushes, so the ship lay right next to the riverbank. We hoisted chests and equipment over to Galne, along with the wounded men, and he sailed down the river with two berserks and a handful of the Jarl's men left standing. Trygg, I and four others stayed behind to search for more survivors. And the Jarl. It was a long night.'

Arngrim looked straight ahead without meeting Vass's eyes. His body trembled as if he had just been pulled out of an icy river. He drank more, in silence. Even Geir Galne was quiet.

'After chasing us back to the river, the Irish turned south to engage Kjetil Korte and his men. It gave us time to free the ship from the tree and pull in the oars that were not broken. The sun was setting when the Irish returned after forcing Kjetil to retreat. The shadows in the woods made it difficult to see, and the enemy moved between the trees, ever closer to us. We could hear them shouting at each other when they found our wounded companions, and we listened as the savages slaughtered them with axes and spears. We recovered four injured and twice as many dead and carried them to Trygg's ship. The Irish found the rest.'

Arngrim rubbed his face and drank to steady himself.

'While the others made the ship ready, Trygg and I ran around in the woods along the north shore and attacked Irishmen where we could find them. The darkness eventually made it difficult to run, and on the way back to the ship for the last time, Trygg stumbled upon a man lying on the ground. It was Bjarn, with a broken arrow protruding from his chest. He was breathing weakly and barely grimaced when we pinched him. All around us were the sounds of running feet and angry voices of the Irish chasing us.'

'Bjarn would not survive the journey down the river, and the Irish would kill him if they found him. Trygg reasoned that they might hesitate if they were not sure he was a Northman. He pulled out the arrow, and we tore off Bjarn's weapon shirt and greaves. We hastily cut his hair and his beard and flung it into the river along with the clothes.'

'Did it work?' Vass asked.

'I do not know,' replied Arngrim. 'Trygg ordered me to steer the ship down the Blackwater and the Boyne while he stayed behind to keep the Irish occupied. Then he disappeared between the trees again.'

'What happened then? Did you reach the Boyne without more encounters with the Irish?'

'Yes, thanks to Trygg's courage and the darkness of the night. The ship took more damage before we reached Øystein Glumra's camp at the mouth of the Boyne. One of his ships had to pull us up here to Linn Duachaill the next day.'

'What about Trygg? How did he get here?'

'We don't know. Trygg showed up here three days later, with Sigurd Jarl's body sewn into a bearskin. Perhaps it took a while to find a bear big enough for the Jarl?' Arngrim smiled for the first time since he had started telling the story.

'That is not exactly how it was.'

Vass looked up. Behind Arngrim stood Magnus Trygg, with Ragnar by his side. The grey-bearded Dane was grinning.

Arngrim apologised. Trygg accepted with a nod, and the two veterans sat down with them. Geir Galne still did not say a word, but now he looked more anxious than drunk.

'Maybe you can tell the story of how you escaped from Kells?' suggested Arngrim to Trygg.

'Better you tell it. It sounds more fun coming from your mouth,' Trygg replied dryly.

Arngrim accepted the reprimand. 'I have been told that Trygg searched the forest through the night until he found the dead Jarl. He had grievous wounds in the stomach and chest. The Irish had taken his weapons and armour and put two men to guard the body. Trygg killed them and dragged the Jarl to the river. There, he removed his own weapon shirt and let the current carry them down the river. He managed to pull the Jarl's body ashore on the south bank of the river and concealed it under the vegetation before the morning sun came out. Trygg spent the following day resting, hiding from the Irish who were still combing the area for survivors.'

Arngrim looked to Magnus Trygg for confirmation but got none. He swallowed before he resumed.

'Before sunset, he found a flimsy vessel made from animal skin. He put the Jarl in the boat and covered it with bushes and leaves. As there was no room for both of them, Trygg had to partly swim and partly hang on to the stern. Several times he had to dive until they had passed Irishmen who saw the boat float by.'

Trygg's face revealed nothing. 'Who told you this?' he asked in a dark and grave tone.

'You did,' Arngrim replied, confused.

Trygg studied him quietly. 'Well, it must be true, then!' he concluded with a small smile.

Ragnar was the first to laugh and eased the tension around the table: 'Hail your brave chieftain!'

'Hail, Magnus Trygg!' the others roared and emptied their drinking horns.

When everybody but Geir Galne seemed to be in a good

mood, Vass dared to ask Magnus Trygg:

'How was the meeting with Torgils today?'

Ragnar immediately became interested, and his face lit up.

The question had the opposite effect on Trygg. 'He told me that he intended to appoint me Jarl of Sygnafylke, after Sigurd.'

The answer was met with quiet wonder. There was something wrong with this. Many would be happy for the wise Magnus Trygg as Jarl, but Trygg himself did not seem the least bit excited. But as far as Vass understood, Torgils had no right to appoint a Jarl among the Northmen.

Geir Galne burst into laughter.

Vass looked at him but decided not to be distracted by the unpredictable berserk.

'What did you answer?' asked Vass.

'No, of course,' Trygg replied.

Galne laughed even louder.

This time, Vass could not ignore him. 'What's so funny?'

'Trygg can never become Jarl of Sygnafylke. He can't even go home!' Geir Galne smiled from ear to ear.

'Shut your beak, old gull!' replied Trygg, without threat or conviction in his voice.

Vass, Ragnar and Arngrim looked from one to the other.

Geir Galne's laughter resounded in the hall.

Suddenly, Trygg got up from his chair and reached for Galne on the other side of the table.

Galne jumped up, with a knife in his hand. The laughter was gone. The berserk, who hitherto appeared drunk beyond sanity, was suddenly alert and ready. And dangerous. He flipped the knife in his hand a few times and stared at Trygg with wide-open eyes.

Magnus Trygg did not spare Galne as much as a glance. He sighed and looked down at the table when he answered the question the others had not dared to ask.

'Galne is right. I can't go home, and I can't be named a Jarl.'

CHAPTER 11: CAMP

The sun hung low when Ulv settled on a new campsite, surrounded by old trees. Here, he could make a fire without any chance that anyone would see the flames. Within a bowshot, there was a stream where he filled the water skin and washed. He had spent a long time cleaning the wound of clotted blood and moss residues. He had indulged in a few mouthfuls of water, but no more. The water tasted fresh, but he would not drink any more until he learned the effect of what he had already consumed. Over the campfire, he dried the cloth he had used to wash with.

He carefully heated the two curved shafts over the fire and straightened them. After repeated cycles of heating and straightening, he had two good arrows.

When the cloth was dry, he used it to wrap new moss over the wound. The makeshift dressing loosened quickly, but it was sufficient to allow him to move carefully around the camp.

By sunset, the fatigued Ulv extinguished the dying fire. Curled up under the cloak between two tufts, he fell asleep with one hand on the seax and the other on the bow.

Sleep was restless. Time and time again, he woke up, believing that the thugs from the camp had found him. He sat upright with the seax pointing in front of him before he was awake. His eyes darted back and forth in search of men who intended to harm him, until he realised that he was alone. He closed his eyes and listened to his pounding heart for a long time before he could sleep again.

Ulv spent a fitful night until he awoke to sunlight through

the leaves. Relieved that it was morning, he sat up and rubbed his face. His empty stomach growled and writhed like a tethered watchdog. It had been a long time since he had eaten properly.

He picked up the two arrows he had straightened the night before. One had bent a little, but at least he had one good and one decent arrow. It would suffice. It had to suffice.

*

Ulv had tracked the animal through the forest for almost half a day. He was spent but getting closer. Luck was with him, as he had the wind in his face as he followed the fresh tracks. Ahead, the forest seemed to open up a little. Ulv crept up behind a bush at the edge of the clearing. Out on the plain, there was a deer with her calf.

Ideally, he should have felled the deer, but he did not risk missing the shot. The calf was closer, but even that shot was difficult from this distance.

Ulv put a knee to the ground and put the best arrow on the string. He breathed a few times, paused, and drew his bow as far as he could muster. Not all the way, but enough for a deadly shot on the grazing calf.

Suddenly, Ulv hesitated. Maybe because he was injured and fatigued. He had eaten too little and slept even less. Maybe because he remembered the shots he had missed in Dyflin. Or perhaps it was something else entirely.

Either way, it suddenly seemed impossible to hit the calf. Ulv lowered his bow and closed his eyes.

'You must not release until you are certain the arrow will kill the prey,' Father whispered.

They sat on a hill and looked down on an elk cow with two calves. Father had taken Ulv on every hunting trip recently, and now it was time for the boy to shoot his first animal.

Training had been time-consuming, and progress was slow.

Still, Ulv had more patience for this kind of practice than anything else. He loved shooting with the bow they had made last winter, and hunting was exciting even when he had not been shooting. Now, it was his turn.

Father had taught him to track and keep the wind in the face when he approached the animal so his scent would not scare the animal before he got close enough.

Again and again, Father had warned Ulv not to approach the animal until he had a good overview of the situation. Even a deceptively placid animal like the elk could be dangerous if threatened. Or even worse: if somebody came between a mother and her offspring.

Father told a story about a hunter who aimed at an elk calf, only to be trampled from behind by the cow. Ulv suspected the story was made up, but he understood the wisdom in telling it.

Ulv and Father had followed the elk tracks for half a day and found themselves ideally positioned downwind from the animals.

'Do you see the calf over there, Ulv?' Father whispered and pointed. 'Can you take it from here?'

'Yes.'

'With a shot that kills it?'

'Yes,' Ulv answered again and drew the bow. He inhaled and aimed high before lowering the bow until the arrow pointed a man's length above the animal.

'Ulv!'

Ulv did not lose his composure. He let fly and held his breath.

The arrow pierced into the cow's flank, just above the front leg. A good shot. The cow wobbled half a dozen steps and dropped dead. Ulv beamed. His body shook with excitement and pride.

Father smiled and clapped Ulv on the shoulder but said nothing. He wasn't happy, and Ulv knew why.

The shot had been a risk for the elk and themselves. If the arrow had missed by just a little, the cow would have been injured. Then they had to follow it to kill the beast so that it would not suffer any more. Ulv had disobeyed Father, and he would hear about it for a long time.

But right now, Father made an effort not to dampen the joy of Ulv's first kill. Ulv felt a sting of shame.

'Great shot, Ulv! Now we shall celebrate your achievement and honour the great animal.' Father said. 'We will deal with the rest later,' he added, with a look that revealed that he was thoroughly looking forward to that.

Ulv opened his eyes. It had been so easy back then. It was just him, the elk cow and the shot. Nothing else mattered. There were lessons in that, in his childish ability to live in the present.

He drew his bow once more. The calf had barely moved. For it was still the calf that was the target. He could push the consequences aside, but he could not take unnecessary chances. After all, he was grown up, and Father could not fix it if things went wrong. His chest rose and fell in a few deep breaths. He aimed high, lowered the arrow until the calf was in sight and let fly the arrow.

A moment later, the calf fell dead.

*

Ulv was full and drowsy. Back at the camp, he had cooked the venison and feasted on the meat to the point of nausea. He feared that he had stuffed himself too much too fast, on an empty stomach.

There was still much to do after the hunt, so he could not sleep. Driven by hunger, he had cut a few pieces of meat as fast as possible. Now remained all the work of skinning, removing the intestines and cutting the meat into strips so that he could dry or smoke it. Despite his condition, there was nothing to do but start the work.

Ulv was well trained, but by no means experienced. The equipment was not the best, either. The skin of the calf turned into some usable pieces, but not into any whole skin. Most of the time was spent carving the meat and hanging it to dry. He settled for quick-drying it over the fire. Not ideal for taste or lastingness, but it was all he could manage.

The night was at an end when Ulv could extinguish the fire and go to sleep. This time, too, he woke up with his heart in his throat and panicked searching eyes, but not as often as last time. He hoped the worst was over.

*

Ulv spent the next couple of days exploring the area in search of a more suitable location for a permanent campsite. The wound was still stiff and sore, but the colour was a natural red. He had water, food and clothes and felt stronger every day.

The nights, on the other hand, had not improved. He spent his night shivering from cold and fear. When he managed to doze off, he would wake up panicked – looking for enemies. The latest nights had been so bad that he did not dare to fall asleep. Despite his fatigue, he welcomed the daylight. It could not continue like this.

Ulv had to return to the men who had attacked him.

CHAPTER 12: FRIDA

Trygg made a gesture towards the bench and waited for Geir Galne to put away the knife before he continued his tale.

'I grew up on my father's farm in Vestfold. We spent our summers as Vikings and filled our coffers with silver. Every year, my father bought more land and employed more servants and thralls. At twenty, I was still not bound to any woman. My father wanted me to marry Hilda, a girl from another wealthy family, as soon as she had come of age.'

'That autumn, I met Frida on our neighbour's farm. She had just married Fritjof, son of old Gisle. Her husband was a rascal who would never amount to anything. He was prone to drinking and did not treat his women well.

'Frida was as gorgeous as Freyja herself. Her black hair smelled like honey and flowers, and her voluptuous figure almost painful to behold.

'You never knew with Frida. Sometimes, she would be decent and proper, to the point of ignoring me. Other times, she would be warm and intimate. At a feast, she put her warm lips to my ear and whispered that she wanted me. She made me know what she would do if she was mine, and I was hers. For years, I was consumed by the battle between desire and jealousy. But I was young and inexperienced, and never dared to believe that I could have her.'

Magnus Trygg looked genuinely dejected. The others listened in silence. Even Geir Galne was quiet.

'We spent a night together, she and I, one summer when her husband was away. It was just as sensational as I had imagined it would be. The next morning her husband returned, and I heard from her no more.

'Frida was the one I wanted but could not get. I met other women, but there was nobody like her. For two winters, I was raiding in the east with the goths. When I returned, I took Hilda as my wife. She was pretty, and wise for her young age. We built our own farm, and she gave birth to our first son. Life was good, for a while.

'While my wife was pregnant with our second son, I met Frida again. She had expelled her pathetic husband, and now she wanted me instead. There was nothing timid or polite about her this time, and I had no strength or will to resist. We spent another night together, better than the first.

'The next morning, I said goodbye to Frida. In the evening, I said goodbye to Hilda. I could not choose between them, and I could not stay with them both. I rode through the night and the next day and boarded a ship to Hedeby.'

Magnus Trygg spoke with his eyes closed. As if he had to make an effort to recall the story. Or unable to look others in the eye. Maybe both.

'Two winters came and went before I returned. I had traded and plundered in the Mediterranean, from Cordoba to Serkland, on Danish and Frankish ships. But I never found peace. Weak in heart and weak in will, I had left my wife and my two sons.

'I was forever in Frida's hold, like a drowned fisherman in Ran's net. I told myself I had no choice: I had to have her. Determined to take Frida as my wife, I sailed for home.'

Many voices chimed in an 'Oooooo!' around the table. Vass had never imagined that the steadfast Magnus Trygg could have experienced something like that or made such choices.

Trygg lifted his gaze.

'I rode straight to Frida. I found her in the yard with a small child in her arms.'

Another 'Oooooo!' morphed into laughter.

'The child was too young to be mine. Frida had taken a new husband. She was never without a husband for long.'

More laughter.

'I rode from Frida in shame and came home to Hilda in the evening. Our reunion was not friendly. My wife thought I was dead and told me she would have preferred just that. While I was away, she had made friends with Frida. Thus, she knew all about my betrayal, and her anger was as painful as her grief.

'Hilda gave me a head start until sunrise before she sent word to her father and brothers that I was back. After giving my two sleeping sons one last kiss, I rode through the night once more. Sigurd Jarl allowed me to join his crew, and I've been his man ever since.'

'Are you an outlaw?' Vass realised it was a stupid question before he had uttered it.

'No, of course not,' replied Trygg, a little annoyed. 'A scorned woman cannot declare a man an outlaw, and her kin did not pursue the matter.'

Ragnar shook his head, smiling. 'I have just met you, Magnus Trygg, but I understand that you are a man of great courage and a big heart. Your name is held in high regard in the north as well as here on the islands. Surely, your women must also have heard about you. There cannot be many men called Magnus in the north.'

Trygg shook his head. 'No, I have never known a Northman to name his son Magnus. Neither did my father. My name is Tryggr. During a trip to Miklagard, I was in the service of a Frankish captain who could not pronounce my name. He called me Tuggr, until he started calling me Magnus. Probably because I was taller than most Franks. I decided to keep that name after I left my two wives. It was safer.'

Ragnar laughed and raised the drinking horn to a toast. 'To your wisdom, Magnus Trygg, even if you got it late in life.'

CHAPTER 13: BELLO GALLICO

'Who is Hel?'

'What?' Bjarn lifted his upper body from the bed, grimaced, and lay down again with a small whimper.

'Who is Hel? You promised to tell me about Hel.'

Marcus sat in a chair under the window, reading a book. His legs rested on the empty bed next to the wall. On the shelf along the short wall between the window and the door were three other books.

'Back on the ship, you told me that ...'

'Tell me where we are!' Bjarn interrupted.

'Ireland'

'Where?'

'The abbey of Kells,' Marcus replied.

'Did we capture the monastery in Kells?' The Northman propped himself up on his elbows. His face revealed a mixture of surprise and hope.

'The monastery captured us,' Marcus replied. He spoke slowly, taking his time with each word.

Bjarn looked around the room and lay back on his back again.

'Where are the others?'

'I do not know. The Jarl is dead. And many more. Some ran to the ships.'

The Northman was silent for a while. 'How did I get here?'

'I do not know. What do you remember?'

Bjarn gently touched his chest and felt the edges of the pieces of cloth that covered the wound.

'The arrow hit me above the lungs?'

'Not too deep,' Marcus replied, 'but the wound was dangerous.'

The injured warrior placed his legs outside the bed and sat up with considerable effort. 'How long ago?'

'Seven days,' Marcus replied.

'We must get back to the others!' Bjarn got up with a grunt, swayed and plopped down on the bed again.

'Must we?' Marcus asked.

Bjarn sent Marcus an angry look. 'Of course! We are not going to stay here and become monks of the White Christ!'

'Better monk than thrall,' Marcus replied quietly.

A knock on the door interrupted the argument. A young man in a grey robe, similar to the one Marcus himself had received, entered the room. He stood in silence for a while, studying Bjarn.

Marcus followed his gaze to the Northman lying on his back on the bed. His eyes were half-open and unfocused, as if trying to look inside his own head. The face was frozen in a pained expression. His breathing was uneven and strained.

The grey-clad novice shook his head slowly. He removed the chamber pot and some bloodstained pieces of cloth Marcus had used to dress the wound.

'Mass at noon,' he said in Celtic.

Marcus had only learned a few Celtic words, but it helped that so many monastic terms were Latin. Mass was one of them.

Marcus nodded, and the young monk walked backwards out the door.

‘Where’s my beard?’ Bjarn asked a moment after they heard the sound of the wooden beam replaced outside the door. He was stroking his chin with his hand.

‘I ...’ Marcus searched for the word, making a scratching motion with an invisible knife against his cheek.

‘Shaved?’ Bjarn suggested.

‘I shaved it. Somebody had ...’ Marcus made a slightly coarser movement with the invisible knife.

‘Cut!’ Bjarn stated.

‘Somebody cut your beard. And hair. Ugly.’

With a dissatisfied grimace, Bjarn nodded and felt what remained of his hair.

‘Why?’

‘I do not know.’

Bjarn was silent. Marcus opened the book again.

During the tour of the monastery with the abbot, they had visited the scriptorium: a room full of books, scrolls and parchments. Cearan let him pick copies of four books while they were there, all in Latin.

Marcus started with the most exciting one. It was easier to read Latin now. He had made a list of words he did not understand and asked Cearan or any other monk when he met them.

He read four pages and added thirteen new words to the list.

‘What are you reading?’ Bjarn sat up again.

‘Bello Gallico,’ Marcus replied. A small smile made its way to his lips.

‘What is it about?’

‘Julius Caesar and the war on the Gauls.’

‘Who is Julius, and where is the war?’ Bjarn made another attempt to get up. This time he was more careful and steadied himself against the wall.

Marcus looked at him and nodded approvingly at Bjarn's efforts. 'Julius Caesar was ...' He stopped, frustrated he did not know the words he needed to complete the sentence. 'He was Roman,' he tried, looking at Bjarn to see if he understood.

Bjarn nodded.

'He was a Roman Jarl, with a large country.' Marcus did not know any other Norse words for an army commander or emperor.

'A king, then?' suggested Bjarn.

Marcus shook his head. 'No, not king. The Romans did not like kings. He was Caesar.'

He looked at the Northman and wondered how he could explain that the Romans would not tolerate kings, and that Julius Caesar was killed when somebody thought he was trying to crown himself king. He gave up and chose the easiest way out.

'Well, Caesar was Roman king.'

Bjarn nodded and smiled.

'What is it called when you win a war and take the land?' Marcus asked.

'Vanquish? Conquer?' suggested Bjarn.

Marcus thought about it before continuing.

'Caesar conquered Gallia Transalpina nine hundred years ago.'

'Where is Gallia?'

'It was west of what we now call the Kingdom of the Franks. Or Francia,' Marcus replied. 'Caesar wrote a book about it. Gallia. Gaul. Wars. Battles.'

'Why are you reading it?'

'To learn Latin.'

That was not the whole truth. Indeed, Cearan had suggested it because it was well suited for learning Latin. More important to Marcus, he found solace in the name of Gaius Julius Caesar. His father's name was Gaius, and his sister's name was Julia. That could not be coincidental. Marcus felt obliged to read this particular book. After a few days of reading, he understood why. The text was full of strategy on how to wage war.

He read about the siege of Alesia at least twenty times, in which Caesar defeated hundreds of thousands of Gauls led by their chieftain Vercingetorix.

He did not want to reveal this to the Northman. Instead, he repeated his initial question:

'Who is Hel?'

This time Bjarn answered.

'Hel is Loke's daughter. Sister of the wolf Fenris, who will devour Odin at Ragnarok, and to the Midgard Serpent, which encircles the world of men.'

'Big worm,' Marcus commented dryly.

'Do you want to hear the story or not?'

'I'm sorry,' Marcus said. It was Ulv who had taught him that word, after admitting to killing his father.

'Hel is half living and half dead. On one side of the face, the skin is smooth and healthy, like that of a beautiful woman. On the other side, the skin is pale and rotten.' Bjarn spoke slowly, allowing Marcus to keep up with the story.

'Hel's realm is Niflheim, farthest north. Most who die will go there, except for those brave men who die in battle. The Valkyries collect the fallen warriors and bring them to Valhall. Upon them is bestowed great honour, and they will fight by Odin's side at Ragnarok. Virgins also end up somewhere else when they die. But the weak and sickly go to Hel. They die without honour. That is why all men fear her.'

Marcus let it sink in. There was a lot he did not understand. The Vikings feared ending up in Hel's realm of death, with the frail and feeble. Only bravery would allow them to enter Valhall instead, and death in battle was the best fate to befall the Northmen. That would explain their preoccupation with war, courage and bravery.

How could anyone defeat an army of mighty warriors who were not afraid to die, who even desired to die in battle?

*

The Mass was a test of patience.

Marcus entertained himself by trying to understand as much Latin as possible. He glanced at Bjarn standing next to him, wearing a grey woollen robe for the occasion. The stout Northman could not understand the hymns or prayers of a god he did not acknowledge, let alone worship. His face was pale, and his legs barely carried the weight of his body.

The only rest they got when they kneeled in prayer. Marcus could discern Bjarn's words, but he assumed they were not among the monastery's common prayers.

When they sat down for the third time, Bjarn leaned forward as he grabbed his chest and groaned in pain. Marcus leaned towards him and whispered:

'Where does it hurt? Do you bleed?'

Bjarn did not answer. Instead, he groaned even louder. Marcus looked up at the congregation for help, but they only offered glares and scowls.

Only when Bjarn rolled from side to side on the stone floor and cried in pain, did the abbot cease the litany.

'It would seem that our two lay brothers need help. Would somebody escort them to their room before we continue the prayer? I'm sure our Lord will understand and sympathise.'

Four novices lifted Bjarn, neither gently nor kindly. Marcus walked in front of them up to the room and opened the door. The monks settled the whining Northman on the bed, pulled off his robe and quietly left the room. This time, there was no sound of a beam reinstated to bar the door from the outside.

Marcus washed his hands before carefully removing the pieces of cloth that covered the injury. The thick, reddish-brown crust was still intact. There was no sign of purulence in the wound. Marcus gently cleaned the skin and replaced the dressing.

'Can you hear me?' he asked the Northman.

Bjarn responded with a slight nod.

'Can you tell me what hurts?'

The answer was barely audible: 'Does not hurt.'

Surprised, Marcus straightened up. 'Not hurt? Why did you cry?'

'It was very boring,' Bjarn replied with a smile.

Marcus resisted the urge to punch him. Barely.

'You will go to Hel!' Marcus turned his back to Bjarn and strode over to the window.

'Maybe, but not today,' Bjarn said.

'We shall see,' replied Marcus, watching three horsemen approaching the monastery.

CHAPTER 14: FINAL VOYAGE

Two hundred men, women and children gathered on the beach at Linn Duachaill to honour the Jarl about to embark on his final voyage. The ship was moored on the north bank of the Glyde, a stone's throw upstream from where the river flowed into the sea.

Vass discerned that it was not the Jarl's ship that was bathed in torchlight in the autumn darkness. Instead, this was Magnus Trygg's ship, filled with dry wood and soaked in oil. The mast and the hull were damaged, and the repairs were not sufficient to make the vessel seaworthy. There were no sails, so the broken mast did not make much of a difference. Nevertheless, Vass frowned at the mockery of denying the Jarl command of his own ship for this last and most important journey. The gods would not be pleased.

Four hirdmen carried their Jarl through the silent crowd on their way to the longship. The thick planks of the broad stairs in front of the ship's side creaked as the escort boarded. The housecarls hoisted the massive Jarl with a joint effort and lay him down on a tall stack of firewood and branches without collapsing it. Vass nodded appreciatively, impressed by the display of strength.

The four hirdmen then picked up torches and returned to the stairs, two on each side. A new procession slowly passed through the crowd. Foremost was a girl who could not have seen more than four winters, carrying a bowl with onions and apples. Then followed two girls and two boys, each child older than the previous, displaying containers with nuts, bread, beer, and mead. Behind them was a woman, whom Vass assumed to be the children's mother, holding a helmet that gleamed in the torchlight.

The last member of the procession was an imposing man with blonde hair, a stern face and a broken nose. Kjetil Korte, whom most people now referred to as Kjetil Flatnose when he was not around. He carried a dog that writhed futilely in his strong arms.

One by one, they boarded the ship and placed their offerings next to the Jarl's body. Each found a torch and lined up with the hirdmen.

Kjetil placed the dog on the ground in front of the stairs but held it back by the scruff with his left hand. With his right, he drew a large sword up from the sheath on his back and lifted it towards the sky. He paused and looked from the dog to the sword and back again.

'Helgi!' said Kjetil, determined.

The eldest boy leapt down from the stairs to stand by his father's side.

'Hold the dog!'

Helgi grabbed the dog by the scruff, as his father had done. But he also knelt in front of it and spoke softly to calm it.

Kjetil seized the moment. He grasped the sword with both hands and swung it against the dog's back and shoulders.

Vass winced from the sounds of crushed bones and gashed flesh. In a battle, that was a wonderful song of victory and glory. In this place, at this moment, it was a hideous noise.

A short whimper, then all was quiet. The dog was split in two. The head, with half the chest and one foreleg, lay on one side, the rest of the body lay on the other side of a boy soaked in blood.

Nearby, a woman howled with delight.

Aud. Of course. The volve relished blood above all else. Vass had seen her paint houses with blood on Sanday. In Dyflin, she smeared the Irish civilians with blood. She was rumoured to have overseen the ritual slaughter of monks in several monasteries. The Irish claimed she had been ecstatic as she painted her naked body with the monks' blood and performed seid on White Christ's altar. Vass did not know the truth, but he had never heard of any other volve serving the gods the way Aud did. She was Torgils's wife, so nobody was tempted to point it out.

Kjetil Flatnose raised his bloodied sword, and the crowd cheered. He pointed to the dog, both halves of it, and ascended stairs with the sword in his hand.

Helgi lifted the dog, one half in each hand, and followed his father. Onboard, he placed the dog at the dead Jarl's feet. Kjetil arranged the sword so that the hilt rested on the Jarl's ample belly. Then, he put his hand on his son's shoulder and led him back to the stairs.

Two men climbed the stairs to address the crowd. One was Torgils, dressed in black. His many necklaces, rings and bracelets glinted with every movement. A mighty chieftain, capable of bribing or intimidating others to do his bidding.

Vass leaned towards Arngrim: 'Who is that with Torgils?'

'Øystein Glumra. The Jarl of Møre.' Arngrim whispered without taking his eyes off the spectacle.

Vass felt his blood rush to his head and was relieved Arngrim did not turn to see him blush. Glumra was Sigrid's father, the beautiful shieldmaiden who'd sparred with her brother the day before.

'Whermh ...' Vass swallowed a lump of nothing that had suddenly grown large in his throat, and tried again: 'Where is Møre?'

'On the other side of the North Sea, and about as far north

as you would want to go.'

Vass pushed his distracting emotions away as the Jarl of Møre spoke in a clear voice.

'Tonight, we bid farewell to Sigurd Jarl before his final voyage. We celebrate his memory, and his victory over the Irish!'

The audience cheered politely. Vass wondered what could have happened in the last few days, which caused the Irish to be defeated. The Danes and Northmen held two fortified camps on the east coast. As far as he knew, the Irish clans still controlled the rest of the island. They were fully capable of throwing the invaders into the sea if they stopped fighting among themselves for a few weeks.

'Before we toast to Sigurd Jarl's memory, I present to you: Torgils, the King of Dyflin!'

Glumra shouted the last words with faked enthusiasm. Torgils's supporters applauded, but many others were silent. There was something wrong with this ceremony, with the whole situation.

The self-proclaimed King of Dyflin turned his attention to the silent portion of the crowd, where Vass stood with Arngrim and the warriors from Horthaland. He raised his hand to quiet his followers.

'Sigurd Jarl was a great man and has left a great void in our world.'

There was a hint of a smile in the corner of Torgils's mouth, barely discernible in the dancing light from the flickering torches.

'A great man,' Torgils repeated. This time, there was no doubt that he was smiling. Scattered objections blended with laughter in the crowd.

Torgils put his left hand on the shoulder of the Jarl of Møre, a step below him.

'Øystein Mørejarl will return to Vestlandet in three days.

He will inform Sigurd's family and his people about the Jarl's death.'

Vass nodded. It was an honourable way to convey the message. He abruptly stopped nodding when it dawned on him that the Jarl of Møre would probably bring his son Ragnvald and the enthralling Sigrid with him.

With his right hand, Torgils grabbed Kjetil Flatnose by the arm and pulled him closer to the Jarl of Møre. Torgils had to take a step to the left, because he could not look over Kjetil's head.

'As the King of Dyflin, I name Kjetil Flatnose as my Jarl! His seat will be here in Linn Duachaill, and he will rule over the South Islands and Ireland north of Boyne!'

The jubilant shouts from Kjetil's handful of supporters failed to conceal the general lack of excitement with the appointment.

Kjetil looked angry, and Torgils allowed him to simmer in the humiliation until the pitiful acclamation subsided. With a nod to somebody in the crowd, he patted the two Jarls on their shoulders. The trio merged with the audience to modest applause. Magnus Trygg entered the makeshift stage and spoke from the lowest step:

'Yes, Sigurd Jarl was a great man, Torgils. He led us to victory in many battles. Every year, he shared the haul with his men, as the custom and honour demands, and kept no more to himself than what was right. The Jarl treated us well and ruled justly. Violent was he in battle, but in peacetime, he was mild. Nothing was ever required of us that we would not willingly give. In his last moment, Sigurd stood alone against a hundred Irishmen, sacrificing himself so his men might live.'

Magnus Trygg's gaze found Torgils.

'Yes, Sigurd Jarl was a great man.'

With that, Trygg disappeared into the crowd.

A tense silence had gripped the gathering, as if nobody

dared say anything after Trygg's speech.

'Sigurd Jarl!' cried a man.

'Sigurd Jarl!' the crowd echoed.

'Beer!' shouted another.

'Beer!' roared the others.

The tension burst with relief and laughter. Soon, barrels of beer and mead were rolled out, and the men were toasting to honour the Jarl and the gods.

As was the custom, several animals were slaughtered and brought onboard. Sigurd Jarl would lack nothing on his final voyage.

Not even his thrall, Vass realised as two of Sigurd's hirdmen dragged a man between them.

Vass recognised Emil, the thrall who always attended the Jarl on his travels. It was not uncommon for a Jarl or a chieftain to bring a thrall or two with him to make the journey more comfortable. Some disapproved of the Jarl's choice of a male thrall for such purposes. Sigurd Rassraggr, somebody whispered. But never when the Jarl or his hirdmen was within earshot.

When a Jarl died, his thralls risked following their master in death. Vass had seen stuporous female thralls, unable to protest or resist. Others had fought desperately to escape, to the amusement of the spectators.

Emil was unwilling to accompany his master. On the top of the stairs, he kicked hard against the ship's rim and managed to tear himself free from his escort. The push sent him in a backward roll down the makeshift stairs. He whirled around on his hands and feet and looked for an opportunity to escape. A handful of warriors rushed forward to grab him. Others laughed.

Vass lost sight of the thrall as he darted into the crowd, followed by the sounds of shouting, beatings and laughter. Soon, four housecarls carried the kicking thrall between them. Aud met them below the stairs, with a knife in her hand. She grabbed Emil's brown hair and pressed the blade against his throat. The audience fell silent while the thrall met the gaze of the woman who was about to take his life.

'Eternal pain and disgrace upon you, Aud the Harlot, daughter of Satan,' the thrall exclaimed and spat in her face.

'Ooooo!' The crowd was delighted by the insult to the king's mistress.

Vass wished for a quick death for the brave and obstinate thrall, but Aud's expression changed from surprise to anger and determination. She turned her back to the thrall and wiped off the spit with the back of her hand.

'Tie him to the mast!'

The housecarls promptly obeyed and bound the slave by his hands and feet to the mast, near the Jarl's body. Aud grabbed a burning torch and boarded the ship.

'Burn!' she said and stabbed the torch in between the oil-drenched branches. Without a second glance at the doomed thrall, she strode down the stairs and away from the riverbank.

The fire spread fast and soon engulfed the Jarl. Emil cried in terror as a gust of wind caused the flames to bite him and ignite his clothes.

The onlookers were quiet. Some turned away. Others left. What was supposed to be a dignified burial turned into a vile spectacle.

Vass unhooked the axe from his belt and walked to the ship. Hot air slapped his face as he chopped the ropes that moored the ship to the stilts on the riverbank. The keel scraped against rocks as the river set the floating pyre in motion towards the sea.

A drawn-out howl of agony rang in Vass's ears as he left the crowd on the riverbank.

CHAPTER 15: COMPANION

Ulv approached Browntooth's camp from the same direction as last time, but instead of arching around to the right, he advanced in a semicircle to the left. His favourite arrow was ready on the string, and the seax hung from his belt. The other decent arrow, which he had finally straightened out properly, he held in his left hand together with the bow.

At dawn, the three brigands slouched around the campfire. Their dog could neither be seen nor heard. Halfway between Ulv and the men, there was a tent. A cart was barely visible at the back of the camp.

Ulv hugged the shadows of an outcrop, effectively out of sight for the men staring into the flames. No guards and no vigilance; they were unprepared for an attack.

On the spot the tilting rock served as a roof, Ulv found the dog. It lifted its head and growled as the stranger approached.

He was by no means small, but probably young. Ulv had seen several hounds like him in Dyflin after the attack. All dead, indicating they fought with the Irish. Those were considerably larger, perhaps on a par with a large man when standing on their hind legs. The wary pup in front of him was not yet half their size.

Ulv glanced at the men by the fire, still chattering and utterly unaware of an intruder in the camp. From his belt bag, Ulv produced a piece of meat from the deer calf he had slaughtered a couple of days earlier. The dog whimpered, raised his head higher and followed Ulv with big eyes as he unwrapped the meat from the leaves.

While the pup was busy devouring the treat, Ulv worked on untying the thick rope. As soon as the dog swallowed the meal, it turned to Ulv and barked.

'Shhh, now. Almost done with this stubborn knot.' Ulv spoke softly and drew the seax to cut the rope.

Another bark.

By the fire, the brigands stopped talking and were looking in the direction of the noise. Ulv crouched and crept towards a tree stump between the dog and the campfire. The pup fell quiet, but soon Ulv heard footsteps approaching in the mud. A man spoke in a threatening tone.

With the seax in his hand, Ulv held his breath and peeked over the edge of the stump. He imagined the three armed thugs surrounding him. If they caught him now, after he had reduced the band from five to three members, his life was forfeit.

The tree stump tilted as a brigand stepped on a protruding root on his way to the dog. Ulv doubted that a man who had spent the evening staring into the flames would detect him, even if he turned to look in his direction. He could not anticipate how the dog would react if somebody attacked his master, even a vile master like this one.

Ulv waited.

The pup lowered its head and whimpered, until a kick to the ribs silenced him. His master did not stop at that but grabbed the rope and lifted the helpless animal by the loop that tightened around its neck. Showered in spittle and harsh words, the dog twisted and gasped and hardly uttered a sound as another kick sent it swinging in a wide arc.

A heartbeat later, the tormentor slumped to the ground. Despite his outrage, Ulv had struck with the pommel, not the blade. He cut the rope where it was tied to a root and twirled it twice around his hand for a solid grip. When he turned to the campfire, he met the eyes of the two remaining brigands. One drew his sword, and the other clutched an axe with both hands, but they did not make a move towards the intruder.

Ulv kept his eyes on them and retreated carefully from the camp. The injured dog offered no resistance but whimpered and limped slowly after the insistent rope. Just outside the camp, Ulv kneeled in front of the dog, stroked him gently and spoke quietly. The dog relaxed and allowed Ulv to carry him in his arms as he walked as fast as he could away from the brigands.

*

'What is your name?' Ulv asked, scratching the pup's chin after it had gulped down the remains of the deer calf.

Ulv removed the rope around its neck and rearranged it into a makeshift harness around the torso and forelegs. He carefully washed the wounds and dressed them with moss and strips of cloth.

The tangled grey and black coat reminded Ulv of Sigurd Jarl.

Jarl was a good name. Quite inappropriate for a dog, of course. Perfect.

'Is your name Jarl? Is it? Are you Jarl?'

Jarl paid little attention to the ramblings of his new master and instead devoted himself to sniffing around for more food.

*

Ulv spent the next few weeks hunting and training Jarl. He had watched as his neighbour, Toralf, trained his hunting dogs, and Father had explained the principles: *Animals learn the connection between something they do and what happens afterwards. If something good happens, they will do it more often. If something unpleasant happens, they will do it less often.*

According to Father, that was pretty much the only rule. And, yes, the consequence should preferably be immediate. Ulv cut small pieces of dried meat to reward Jarl when he did things right. And with that as a starting point, the training commenced.

Ulv saw little use for tricks such as sitting or greeting with his paw, but found it was best to start with something simple. Thus, he trained Jarl to sit on command. Every time Jarl sat down when he was supposed to, he received a piece of meat. Later, he had to remain sitting for a while to get the reward.

They made slow progress at first. Frustratingly slow. Perhaps because the pup had received little or no training in the first months of his life, or perhaps because Jarl still did not fully trust that a human cared for him. But gradually, as the dog was fed and recovered from his wounds, his performance in training also improved. Soon they could work on more complicated commands, where Jarl would stay somewhere or be completely silent.

Their hunting also went well. There was abundant wildlife in the area. In the beginning, Ulv had to leave Jarl behind long before he approached the prey. Later, there was a period where they had to learn not to ruin the hunt for each other. Jarl was not great at tracking, but he had good hearing and could pick up an animal's scent long before Ulv could see it.

Soon, Jarl caught hares on his own and joined his master when hunting larger animals. Sometimes, he was too eager and started chasing down animals that Ulv had sneaked up to shoot. The once emaciated dog was now healthy and robust. Jarl consumed vast amounts of meat, so their food stores were meagre. Ulv enjoyed his invaluable company too much to mind the missed opportunities and meals.

The nights also improved, as Ulv trusted that Jarl would warn him of any danger or uninvited guests. But even with this vigilant guard, Ulv would wake up in a state of panic, convinced that he was under attack. This constant sense of danger was the decisive argument for Ulv's decision to move. Equally important, they would need a better campsite to survive winter.

An enemy of the Irish and an outlaw among the Northmen, Ulv could not rely on anyone's kindness or charity.

Ulv figured that he might as well go north, increasing the distance to the brigands. Also, it would take him closer to Marcus. If his former slave was still alive, he was probably somewhere north of Dyflin. Marcus had been with Sigurd Jarl, Geir Galne and the others up the river, which lay northwest of Dyflin. When Galne and Kjetil Flatnose returned to Dyflin, Marcus was not with them.

North of Dyflin, there were groups of Northmen and Danes who might not know Ulv was outlawed. During the cold nights, he contemplated the prospects of spending winter in a warm bed with a roof over his head.

Satisfied with the decision, he prepared for the journey. Their hunts had provided him with some good hides and furs. He had become better at taking care of the skins from the animals he had killed, and the last ones had been quite nice.

When he was not hunting, training Jarl or trying to sleep, Ulv spent his time shooting with his bow. Ragnar's warriors had described how the previous owner had placed the arrow on his thumb on the right side of the bow, allowing him to shoot much faster than usual. Ulv practised this when he had the opportunity. It felt unnatural, but the benefits were so evident that he kept rehearsing. The precision was still lacking, but he could already shoot faster than before.

At the same time, he trained Jarl to lie still and be quiet, which was challenging for the dog – especially if there was prey nearby. But the distractions made for even better learning, and Ulv welcomed the opportunity to shape Jarl into an even more reliable hunting partner.

However, the hunting and archery practice created a new problem: Ulv was running out of arrows. He could always make new shafts, but he could not forge new arrowheads. It was only a matter of time before they were gone.

After the attack on Browntooth's camp, he'd been down to the three arrowheads. Although he searched carefully every time a shot did not hit its mark, two of them were now gone, leaving only one arrow.

It was no longer possible to postpone the plan. Ulv must break camp and find a more suitable place.

CHAPTER 16: MUSHROOMS

'Is it edible?'

Julia lifted the mushroom to her face and sniffed it. There was no odour. That was unusual. Most mushrooms smelled of something.

'What does it smell like?' asked the woman behind her.

'Nothing,' Julia replied, hesitantly. She held out her hand and waited for the blind woman to locate her arm in the air.

Cwen's sinewed fingers found Julia's forearm, pulling it towards her so she could smell the mushroom. Her leathery skin was covered in scars.

'Useless girl! A dead owl would pick up the scent from the other side of the bog!'

Julia grimaced. She always messed up, and Cwen always let her know that she was too sloppy. Too slow. Too heavy. Too noisy.

'But this particular mushroom doesn't smell much,' Cwen continued, her nose wrinkling below the filthy strip of cloth that covered her eyes. 'Tell me what it looks like.'

Julia tilted her head as she tried to comprehend whether this was Cwen's way of admitting she had not made a mistake after all. It had happened before on the rare occasions Julia had lived up to her expectations. She might say something that almost sounded nice. Once, Cwen announced that Julia might learn to do a few things right if she lived long enough.

'Damn you, laggard! Tell me about the mushroom. Describe it to me.'

Julia swallowed the notion of Cwen trying to be kind.

'The hat is light brown, with pale warts close together. It has gills and a white ring. The stem is thicker at the base, with a reddish colour. Almost pink.'

Cwen pushed her hand away with an indifferent expression. 'You can eat it if you want.'

Julia retracted her hand and smelled the mushroom again.

'But I would not,' Cwen continued, turning her straight back to the girl.

Julia looked up, surprised. 'Why not?'

'Because I intend to live a little longer.'

Julia threw the mushroom away and bent to rub her hands clean in the grass. 'Thank you. What is it called?'

'I have never heard a name,' Cwen replied, 'but I know that anyone who eats that will not live to see three sunsets.'

'How do you know?'

'I prepared a stew of those for my second husband,' Cwen replied.

Julia closed her eyes and took a deep breath. 'Why did you do it?'

'Because I was angry with him.'

'Why were you angry?'

'Because he beat me. He yelled at me, pulled my hair and kicked me. And worse.'

Cwen bowed her head. A tangle of black, unkempt hair fell over her shoulders and curtained her face.

They walked in silence back to the shelter they had shared since the Vikings attacked Wucestre and took everything away from Julia – except for her knife she utilised to kill the blonde raider who chased her through the woods.

On that fateful day, Julia had tried to reach the hut in the marshes. Her broken left arm throbbed with pain with every heartbeat, and she did not walk far until she succumbed to cold and despair. She lay on her back and looked up at the sky. The wind carried grey smoke from the burning village. It was all quiet, and Julia closed her eyes to sleep. To die.

She had been awakened by the touch of Cwen's cold hand on her forehead. The old woman whispered as she examined her. Julia lay still until Cwen began to squeeze down towards her left elbow. 'No,' she said, and tried to retract her broken arm. The movement caused a wave of pain to wash over her, and she could not help but scream.

'A broken arm,' the woman had stated. 'I thought it was something serious, with all this blood. Lie still, and I'll find something to tie it up. When we get home, I have something for the pain as well.'

Cwen had said no more. She used leaves to dress the wound, and with branches, twigs and strips of cloth, she bound Julia's arm to her chest, so she was able to walk without passing out from the pain. Every step was excruciating, but she managed to follow the woman north towards the marshes, by the same route she had planned to escape from the Vikings. Marcus was right about the hut in the swamp. It was Cwen's home, and Julia's for the last two months.

The earthen hut was located on a hill with an overview of the surrounding marshes. A protruding rock served as a wall and roof for the north-western part of the shelter. The mud and turf hand dug out from the floor had been used as building materials for the other walls, packed tightly and bound with twigs and roots. Several layers of braided branches made up the rest of the roof, providing some protection from the wind. When it rained, only the part covered by the stone ledge was dry. The fireplace was a ring of stones by the outer wall, and the smoke rose through the roof. The hole in the wall that served as an entrance was usually open, but they would cover it with a door of braided branches in miserable weather. The beds were made from twigs, dried grass and animal skins. There was not much space for the two women, but it would make it easier to keep warm through the winter.

Julia had decided to return to Wucestre when her left arm was healed. She still kept it in a sling tied to the body, mainly to protect it from bumps and unintended movement. Several times a day, she unbound it and moved it around gently. Both the wound and the fracture seemed to heal well. Cwen knew what she was doing when she took care of her.

The woman in the mud hut owned almost nothing. Still, she shared what she had, even in the face of a long winter and a scarcity of food. Therefore, Julia was grateful and never complained.

With her right arm cradling the left, Julia took a few quick steps until she could walk next to Cwen. There was something in her story that did not fit.

'How did you know this particular mushroom would kill your husband?'

'I tried several until I found one that worked.'

'Did he not get sick from some other mushrooms?'

'Yes, but he did not die until he ate the one with warts.'

Julia accepted the explanation. 'How many men have you had?'

'What do you mean? How many have I lived with, or how many have I slept with?'

'Lived with!'

'Oh, then.' Cwen seemed almost disappointed. 'Only two others.'

'What happened to them?'

'They died.' There was no trace of sadness in her voice.

'What did they die of?' Julia feared the answer.

'They ate mushrooms.'

Julia let it sink in. The woman she lived with had killed three men and lived to tell the tale. 'Did nobody accuse you of killing them?'

Cwen took a deep breath before answering. 'Yes, eventually, they did. But I did not wait for them to figure it out. When my third husband exhaled for the last time, I packed what I could use and hid in the woods. Before long, I found this hut where I survived five winters. If the townspeople find us, they will kill me.'

A thin, crooked finger pointed at Julia. 'And you!'

CHAPTER 17: SONS OF KINGS

A knock on the door signalled the end of an eternity of waiting. Abbot Cearan himself came for him. Before they left, he replaced the bar, confining Bjarn in the room. Neither Cearan nor Marcus uttered a word as they passed through the monastery courtyard. In the otherwise empty refectory, they met with the three men who had arrived at noon.

'Marcus, allow me to introduce you to the high-born of the Cholmáin clan. This is Flann, son of King Ruanaid of Meath.' Cearan indicated with an open palm towards a red-haired man with a narrow face. Marcus assumed that the man had seen twice as many winters as himself. He looked harmless.

Cearan moved his arm slightly, pointing to a tall, slender figure. Marcus's heart stopped in his chest when he recognised the Irish warrior who had killed Sigurd Jarl, and was ready to execute Marcus as well. Now, he got another chance to finish that task.

'This is Sechnall, Flann's brother. You have met before.'

Marcus bowed to the Irishman, avoiding his gaze.

'And here is Diarmait, son of the late High King Conchobair, brother of Ruanaid. These three men are our future.'

The slim man nodded slightly, while his unnaturally dark eyes examined Marcus. Raven-black hair was oiled and combed from one side and hung over his right ear. Neatly trimmed sideburns reached down to the angle of the jaw.

Marcus felt a firm hand on his shoulder and was half led, half dragged to the middle of the room.

'This young man calls himself Marcus, and declares he is the son of a merchant from Northumbria. He claims he was a slave on board the Viking ships that rowed up the River Blackwater ten days ago.'

Marcus noticed the words he *declares* and *claims* and was surprised that the abbot spoke that way. The abbot seemed to believe the story from day one. Now, he withdrew his support and abandoned Marcus to the judgement of the Irish nobles.

Marcus found himself suddenly incapable of speaking, or even thinking. Mouth open, he looked questioningly at Cearan. The abbot tilted his head and seemed not to understand.

'I do not speak their language,' Marcus said.

Cearan smiled.

'We will have to remedy to that. For now, we can converse in Latin. These sons of kings received their education at the monastery in their youth and speak several languages.'

Marcus had underestimated the Irish. He stammered an apology and forced himself to meet their eyes. The dark Diarmait scrutinised him with a blank expression. There was a hint of a smile under Sechnall's moustache. Marcus could not understand what he thought was amusing and dreaded finding out.

'Why do you live?' The Latin words Sechnall used were right, but it was easy to hear that he did not speak Latin often.

Marcus did not have a good answer and needed time to determine the unfamiliar expressions. While he pondered, the silence became oppressive, and Sechnall's smile disappeared.

'I was worth more as a slave than as a dead man,' Marcus said, hoping his Latin words conveyed their intended meaning.

'Were there other slaves on board?'

Sigurd Jarl brought his thrall when they attacked

Wucestre, but Marcus had not seen him after arriving at the Orkneys. There could be thralls on some of the supply ships following the Viking raiding fleet. Marcus dismissed those considerations as irrelevant.

'No, I saw no other slaves.'

Another silence.

'Is it common for slaves to be provided with weapons?' asked Sechnall.

'No, I do not think so.' Marcus's voice was shaky, and he could not meet their gazes. The silence was chilling, as if he was standing wet and naked, exposed to the northern wind. He could not endure it.

'My master fell into the sea at Hoy. I offered to fight in his place because I feared that the crew would sacrifice me to their false gods in exchange for good sailing conditions.'

Even more silence.

'So, you chose to fight alongside the invaders against us?' Flann no longer seemed harmless.

'No! I did not fight against you! I did what I had to survive until I had a chance to escape!'

'You lied to the Northmen to save yourself?' The left corner of Flann's mouth pulled up into a crooked smile. The kind of smile you make when you hear a story you know to be a lie.

'No. Or, yes. I guess I did.' Marcus had never thought that about it like that.

'Do you often lie to save yourself?' Diarmait's voice was coarse, and Marcus felt an urge to cough to clear his throat.

'No! I never lie!' Marcus was frustrated by being portrayed as a liar. His father had raised him to be an honest man. Liars had no honour. It was only at the monastery it became difficult to tell the truth all the time.

'Only occasionally, when it suits you? I understand. That's how it is for most people.' Now Diarmait also smiled. A smile without a hint of kindness. The narrow lines around the eyes, as if somebody had drawn with charcoal on his skin, made him look all the more menacing.

'No, I did what was necessary to survive!' Marcus found new strength in that belief.

'Did you fight any Irish?' This time it was Sechnall who asked, his facial expression revealing nothing.

'No.' As he uttered the word, Marcus remembered that he had almost run into an Irishman and struck him with the axe shaft as he passed. It did not count as a fight, so he chose not to mention it.

'We discovered a wounded man by the river after the battle. He wore no armour or insignia and was unable to account for himself. An arrow, of the type the Northmen used, lay in his hand, and he was bleeding from a wound in his chest. We could not let him die without making sure he was not Irish. That's why we brought him here. You took care of him. Do you know who he is?' Sechnall assumed command of the conversation.

'Yes,' Marcus replied.

'Is he a Northman?'

Marcus feared that he was about to sentence Bjarn to death.

'I think so,' he replied hesitantly – another lie.

'Do you know the man?' asked Sechnall.

'Not very well.'

'Have you seen him before?'

'We were on board the same ship on our way up the Blackwater,' Marcus replied.

'Why do you say you think he's a Northman when you know him to be?'

Marcus had regretted the lie the moment he said it. He was risking his own life to save Bjarn's.

'The wounded man has crossed the North Sea, but I do

not know if he is a Northman or a Dane. It is difficult for me to tell them apart.'

With difficulty, he recovered from the slip, and some of his courage returned.

'We have to ask him, then,' Sechnall concluded. 'Can he ride?'

Marcus was unprepared for this development.

'No, he's still weak. He has fainted several times, from exhaustion and loss of blood.'

He omitted to add that Bjarn usually collapsed from boredom, and always recovered remarkably fast. So many lies.

'Will he reject the heathen gods and turn to the true faith?' Cearan interjected.

Marcus hesitated. There was nothing about Bjarn or his countrymen that indicated that any of them would renounce their gods. To the Northmen, White Christ was a weak god, and his followers were easy prey.

But, if Marcus said that, the abbot would leave Bjarn to the dubious mercy of the Irish.

'Who hath known the mind of the Lord? How unsearchable are His judgments, and untraceable His ways!' Marcus recited, closing his eyes and lowering his head as if in prayer. It was difficult to imagine a graver sin than lying to an abbot by quoting the Letter to the Romans to save a heathen invader.

Cearan nodded approvingly, but Diarmait lost his patience:

'We have not brought an enemy here to be initiated as a monk! Either we take him with us now, or he dies before the sun sets!'

Marcus saw a chance and seized it. 'The Northmen are stubborn and brave. He will not reveal anything worthwhile to you. But he can tell me, and I know his language and his people well enough to understand him. I can alert the abbot when I learn something important, and he can send for you.'

The imposing Sechnall advanced two steps and placed a firm hand on each of Marcus's shoulders.

'I will return in three moons, and you will tell me what you have learned. If the Northman escapes, you die in his place.'

CHAPTER 18: NORTH

Ulv and Jarl watched the activity in Dyflin from behind a tree trunk. There was still work going on with fortifications and ramparts, and the town seemed much more like a stronghold now than earlier in the autumn. Ulv was about to withdraw to let Jarl roam around in the forest. It had cost many pieces of meat to keep the impatient dog still. Ulv stroked his companion's neck and whispered to him when he spotted a man heading for the woods. With Jarl in tow, Ulv grabbed his belongings and snuck between the trees, searching for a place where he could talk to the lone stranger without drawing attention from anyone else.

Satisfied, he whistled softly and waved at the stranger. The man stopped and looked around. He wore grey wool trousers and a green tunic, a bow over his shoulder, an axe and seax in his belt. Calmly, he unhitched the bow from his shoulder and approached Ulv with a confident demeanour. His hair was fair, and his beard was cut short.

'Good morning, friend,' said Ulv, when the man was only ten steps away, wagering a guess the stranger was a fellow Northman.

'Good morning,' replied the man in Norse, nodding briefly before he glanced down at Jarl.

Jarl growled softly and bared his teeth.

'I have some fine skins and furs here, and I'm looking for a trade,' said Ulv, gesturing at the bundle by his side. 'I don't ask much in exchange. A quiver with arrows, a whetstone, a cooking vessel, a bucket or a small trough, and a mug.'

'That might not be much, but it's still more than any man would carry around,' replied the stranger. 'The town is open for trade. Just go there, and I'm sure you'll find somebody who will buy your skins.'

'I don't think it is wise. I left town for a reason.'

'Yeah?'

'Yes, let's just say I insulted somebody with the company I kept,' Ulv continued, implying he was leaving Dyflin because of some trivial incident or quarrel.

The stranger answered by raising one eyebrow.

'Now, you stand to benefit from my misfortune, with an opportunity to make an exceptional deal,' Ulv said and stooped to unwrap the furs for display.

'Very well, we can meet here tonight, right after dark, and I'll bring what you need.'

Their agreement sealed by a solemn nod, Ulv repeated the list of equipment before he watched his trade partner return to Dyflin.

Ulv and Jarl could only wait.

*

At dusk, Ulv returned with the bundle of furs in his left hand and the rope with Jarl in his right. They had not waited long before the dog growled and stared into the twilight in the direction of the village. Soon, Ulv could discern the approaching figure, with a bow over his shoulder and a bulging sack in his left hand. The Northman raised his hand for a greeting. Ulv glanced over his shoulders to see if he was alone but settled on relying on Jarl to alert him if others were lurking around.

'I brought your things,' said the man, tossing the sack in front of him. 'But something tells me that I would have been better paid by Kjetil Flatnose if I brought you to town.'

Ulv tried to suppress a smile. Had the nickname he had given Kjetil stuck with him?

The smile faded as Ulv focused on the risky situation at hand. The warrior had thrown the sack with the equipment right in front of him, waiting for Ulv to pick it up. That would provide the ideal opportunity for a sudden attack. But if that was his intention, why would he reveal he knew about Ulv's predicament? Maybe he was not sure and looked for a reaction?

Ulv glanced at the sack on the ground. Did it contain his supplies, or something else entirely?

Jarl snarled, and Ulv looked up at the man standing with one hand behind his back. Ulv's right hand released Jarl's rope and drew the seax from his belt. The two men stood staring at each other.

'I do not know what you know or think you know,' Ulv said, 'but Kjetil Flatnose won't reward you for dragging me back to town. It was Flatnose who expelled me. He wants revenge on my thrall, and he's not with me, as you can see.'

The Northman stood still and looked at Ulv with his right hand behind his back. Jarl barked, and advanced to stand between his master and the stranger.

'Consider if it's worth it. I will not come voluntarily, and even if you defeat me, there is still my friend here to contend with afterwards.'

Ulv nodded at Jarl, who moved even closer and snarled towards the man. 'Maybe you've seen a dog like this in battle before? He will never give up. Not until one of you is dead. Down that path lies a poor deal for all of us. Don't go there.'

The Northman glanced at the fierce dog baring his teeth a few steps in front of him.

'Calm down, boy,' said the warrior. 'I was just going to get the mug for you,' he continued, and with slow movements, he unhooked a drinking mug from his belt and dropped it on to the rucksack.

'Throw the furs to me, and we're all going to be fine.'

Ulv would have preferred to examine the sack for its contents first but opted to resolve the tense situation before somebody went at the other's throat.

He spoke softly to Jarl before he threw the bundle. The Northman caught it, nodded briefly and turned. Strapped to his back was a broad knife of the type he had seen Geir Galne use for a throwing knife. Ulv exhaled in relief while he watched the warrior return to the town.

'Come, Jarl.' Ulv grabbed the sack and the rope and slipped into the woods.

CHAPTER 19: FAREWELL

Julia awoke from haunting dreams. Or haunting memories. She was curled up in her brother's arms in the cellar. Marcus held her head close to his chest to muffle her sobs and covered her ears so she would not hear what was happening above the floorboards separating the children from their mother.

The Vikings had kicked in the door moments after their mother closed the trap door to the cellar. They did not kill her. Julia could still hear her mother's voice:

'Stay there! Completely still!'

Again and again, accompanied by coarse laughter. Mother cried and screamed, for what seemed an eternity, until Julia ran out of tears. When all was quiet, their mother was gone.

Julia arose halfway from her bed in the cramped hut. Quietly, so as not to wake Cwen, she set foot on the ground and slid out of bed. She braved the cold outside to relieve herself. The rime thawed under her bare feet. Soon, the sun would rise to what seemed to be a clear and cold day.

Cwen was awake when she returned to the cabin. 'You are as stealthy as a storm in a forest of dry leaves!' she said. Cwen always complained that she was making noise. Maybe her hearing was better because she could not see? Julia had learned to move almost soundlessly, but it was never enough.

Nevertheless, she was grateful to Cwen for giving her a

chance to survive. Her left arm was still sore, but the bones were mending, and the wound did not fester. In time, it would be fine, Cwen said.

'What are we going to eat?' Julia asked as she looked around.

Until a few weeks ago, the woods abounded with small animals and plants. As autumn turned into winter, it was more challenging to find enough berries or edible mushrooms. It was not tempting to stand in the freezing river in the hope of catching a stray fish that had not yet sought deeper water for the winter. They encountered deer and wild boars but had no weapons to kill them. Their simple snares and traps were empty.

'We'll go out and see if we can find anything,' Cwen replied. She did not seem angry, just worried.

'What happens when winter comes, then?' asked Julia.

'It gets a lot worse,' Cwen replied.

'How did you manage through the winters, then?'

'I'm old and do not need much food when I'm in bed most of the time. The forest provided me just enough to survive.'

'But I'm just a girl. I don't need much food, either!'

Cwen chuckled. 'You're as tall as I, and your bottom is broader already. You're still growing, and your body needs more food.'

'But then I can't be here! We're going to starve to death, both of us!'

'Yes, we will,' Cwen stated.

Julia lay down on her bed again and put her arm over her eyes to shut the world out.

When the sun rose, Julia had made her decision. She was already wearing all the clothes she owned. Her knife was attached to a piece of rope tied around her narrow waist. Looking around the hut, she found that there was nothing else that was hers. She had lost the blanket, the axe and the long knife when she fled Wucestre.

'Thank you very much, Cwen. I will never forget what you have done for me.'

Cwen got up and embraced Julia. She had never done anything like that before. Julia could feel something wet against her cheek. Hesitantly, she put her arms around the skinny body bent under the low roof.

'Wait,' Cwen said, disentangling herself and stooping to rummage around in a small basket. She picked up a leather purse and put it in Julia's hand.

'Flint and steel, a tinderbox and a whetstone. Without fire, you will freeze to death at night. And a knife is a dangerous weapon in the hand of a woman. Keep your blade sharp, always.'

Julia nodded and left while she still had the strength to do so.

On her way back across the marshes towards Wucestre, she thought of Cwen. She might not have been mean after all, even though she had yelled at Julia a lot. The older woman had tried to harden her, to give her a chance to survive alone. She must have known that they would part ways when winter came. Maybe she had tried to scare her away, too. Thinking about it felt both good and bad.

Overwhelmed by the urge to return to the only woman in the world who cared for her, Julia turned and started running back towards the hut. It felt just right, for a short while. She imagined the cold winter, the wind blowing freezing rain through the roof of the cabin, while they lay and held each other until they died from cold or hunger. Her steps slowed down until she stood still, tears flowing. There was no hope for her in the swamp. She turned again and resumed her journey to the south.

Julia had hoped to find the axe, knife and blanket she had lost when she fled Wucestre, but when she reached the area where the Viking and the dog had attacked her, everything was unfamiliar. The forest seemed different at this time of year, and during her flight, she had not kept track of where she was.

The cold breeze made her skin numb under the thin clothes. On her way from the marshes, she had walked so fast that she kept warm. But when she slowed down to search for her lost equipment, she began to freeze. When she started to shiver, she gave up the search.

She found no suitable places to ford the river without getting wet, so she undressed and carried her clothes over her head as she waded into the icy water. Her body shook, and her teeth chattered as she put her clothes back on the other side of the river.

But now, she was almost there. She would find shelter and warmth in Wucestre. Somebody must have survived.

CHAPTER 20: MAXIMUS

Two moons had passed since Marcus met the Irish nobles, but neither Sechnall nor anyone else had asked for news. There were rumours of unrest between the clans again, but nobody in the abbey knew what had happened. The abbot and the monks were upset by the news that Torgils had looted another monastery on the west side of the island. His witch had allegedly desecrated the sacred altar by performing unspeakable pagan rituals. Marcus could easily imagine the scene, but he opted not to inform the monks about his encounter with Aud.

Marcus and Bjarn enjoyed much freedom at the monastery. As long as they attended the masses, they were allowed to spend the rest of the time more or less as they wished. Marcus spent his free time reading books and practising the languages, and he had begun to help the monks make copies and translations of scrolls and scriptures. He spoke Norse with Bjarn and Celtic with the monks.

For Bjarn to recover his strength and agility after the injury, they volunteered for physical tasks like felling trees, chopping wood and repairing the walls. The Northman grew ever more robust, and his habit of faking fits subsided.

However, for the past few weeks, Marcus had been in the scriptorium from morning to nightfall, barely taking time to eat. The monks had allowed him to read the transcripts of Bede and Gildas, Scholasticus, Tacitus, Nennius and Alquin, and several scrolls with Latin translations from Greek and Anglo-

Saxon, and notes of Celtic and Welsh legends. Now, he could read and write without difficulty, and the monks were eager to help with anything he did not comprehend. Some of them recounted tales and legends that were not yet committed to paper.

It all began when Marcus read Bede's account of the Roman emperors and their representatives in Britain. He was tired of emperors when he had come to Gratian, the fortieth emperor after Augustus, who in the year 377 had been emperor for six years. Marcus's heart had jumped up in his throat as he read:

'At which time, Maximus, a man of valour and integrity and worthy of being an emperor, had he not broken the oath of allegiance that he had taken, was made emperor by his army. He passed over into Gaul, and there by treachery, slew the Emperor Gratian.'

Magnus Maximus – Marcus's ancestor – had been a Roman emperor!

Since then, Marcus had read everything he could find about Maximus. The monks had helped him find other texts that told the story of Britain in Maximus's time, and he was soon immersed in texts. For the first few days, Marcus was frustrated by the numerous differences and contradictions in the various texts.

Maximus was not an esteemed character among the monks who had translated the history. Gildas named him a usurper and traitor and blamed him for the weakening of Britain and subsequent conquest by the Jutes and the Saxons.

In Wales, on the other hand, there was a different legend about Maximus, The Dream of Macsen Wledig, in which he was portrayed as the ancestor of the royal family. The more he read, the better Marcus understood who Magnus Maximus had been.

With his head full of names and tales, he sat on the bed after vespers and examined the signet ring Maximus had carried. He pondered the significance of the inscription VIRTVS

ROMANORVM. *Romanorum* meant Roman, or more precisely, of the Romans. *Virtus* was harder to determine. It could mean virtue or represent all the Roman virtues. Was there a particular virtue important to the emperors, such as courage or strength? The Courage of the Romans, perhaps?

'What's so special about that ring?' Bjarn asked.

Marcus had to think before he could answer. How was he to explain to Bjarn who his ancestor was?

'Do you remember the Picts, Bjarn?' he began.

'Do I remember them? I fought them at Fortriu in Pictland three winters ago! We killed two of their kings, at the cost of many good men,' replied Bjarn.

Marcus was surprised by the answer. Magnus Trygg had mentioned a battle when they passed the north coast of Pictland on their way to Ireland, but he did not know that Bjarn had participated.

'I did not know that. But then at least you know the people who live north of the walls of Britain?'

'Which walls?' Bjarn asked.

'The walls of Hadrian and Antoninus,' Marcus replied. 'When the Romans were in Britain, they never managed to defeat the Picts in the north. So, they built long walls to prevent the Picts from attacking the Roman province in the south.'

'When was this?'

'About seven hundred years ago,' Marcus replied.

'Thrilling,' said Bjarn and yawned for good measure, 'but what has that got to do with the ring?'

'Quite a lot. My village was located between these two walls, just north of Hadrian's wall. So, I grew up on the border to the land of the Picts.'

'Have you been attacked by Picts, then?'

'No, our village has only been attacked by Northmen,' Marcus replied. 'But five hundred years ago, the Picts and the

Irish attacked Britannia again and again. The Roman legions were no longer able to repel them, and some of them even cooperated with the Picts and shared the spoils after the raids.'

'Clever!' Bjarn interjected.

'Perhaps. But at this time, my ancestor Magnus Maximus was appointed Dux Britanniorum, leader of the legions of the Roman Empire in the north. He was a skilled army commander, and in several battles, he fought the Picts, Scots and Irish who ravaged the province.'

'What does that mean?'

'What do you mean?' Marcus asked.

'What does Magnus Maximus mean?'

'Well, Magnus means great, and Maximus means greatest …'

'Best name I ever heard!' exclaimed the Northman. 'Did he come from your village too?'

'No, he came from Hispania and had been a Roman senator before coming to Britain.'

'What is a senator?'

'Some kind of a Jarl, or a councillor,' Marcus replied. He had learned that it was not so important that everything was entirely accurate when he explained something to Bjarn. 'Maximus repelled the enemies and subjugated Britannia, and he became the most powerful man in the province. In the year 383, the legionaries appointed him emperor of the Western Roman Empire.'

'He became a king, then?'

'Yes,' Marcus confirmed. 'The problem was that the Romans already had several kings. Therefore, Maximus took an army of legionaries and Britons across the channel to Gaul.'

'The Kingdom of the Franks!' Bjarn was more invested in history now.

'Correct! The army conquered the kingdom of Armorica,

which has since been called Brittany. Then, Maximus marched southeast. At Lyon, he defeated Emperor Gratian and killed him.'

'Gratian was the other king?' Bjarn asked.

'Yes, one of them. In Austria, Theodosius was emperor, or king if you will. He recognised Maximus as emperor of the west. But in the year 388, Theodosius attacked with great force. He defeated Maximus in two battles and executed him. Maximus's only son, Flavius Victor, was killed a few months later.'

'That was the end of that story,' sighed Bjarn.

Marcus reached out to Bjarn and gave him the ring.

'No, the story does not end with the death of his only son. Maximus was married to Princess Elen of Wales. Their daughter, Sevira, married Vortigern, the Briton king of Wales, and Maximus's lineage passed on through their sons ...'

'Another king!' exclaimed Bjarn.

'Yes, but Vortigern does not have a good reputation,' Marcus replied.

'Why not?'

'Because he lost Britain. After Maximus's death, the Roman legions disappeared from the province. The Picts and Scots resumed their raids, and Vortigern had no force to stop them. Therefore, he recruited Jutes, Angles and Saxons as mercenaries. Tens of thousands of them came across the channel each year, and eventually, Vortigern lost control of Britain. He was forced to give the leaders of the mercenaries their own kingdoms in Britain, and these new peoples displaced the Britons.'

'Vortigern was not a good king,' Bjarn stated.

'No, he made many mistakes,' Marcus replied. 'But decades later, the greatest of the Briton kings fought the Anglo-Saxon forces. His name was Ambrosius, but he later became known as King Arthur. He installed Maximus's grandson, Pascent, as King of Wales. From him came the royal family, and the Briton kings who followed him wore Magnus Maximus's signet ring.'

'How did you get the ring, then?'

'My father gave it to me,' Marcus began, but stopped when he realised that not the case. He could not bear to tell how he had seen it in Kjetil Korte's hand and later found it in Ulv's seaman's chest. There was too much in that story he did not know. 'The ring has been an heirloom of the Briton kings, passed from father to son for half a thousand years. My father wore it when he was killed. Now I wear it, as the oldest male of our kin.'

Bjarn lay back on the bed and was quiet for a while before he said anything.

'So, the thrall Marcus is a descendant of a Roman king and a Briton royal family?'

'So it seems,' Marcus replied, unable to suppress his smile.

'Impressive!' said Bjarn and flicked the ring back.

There was a knock on the door the moment Marcus caught the ring in the air. Before he could answer, the monk Brennan entered.

'The abbot will see you. Now!'

'Why?' Marcus asked as he straightened up.

'The king is dead! The clans are at war!'

CHAPTER 21: SWORD

Julia reached the village of Wucestre before dark. Running along the Wansbeck brought warmth back in her body, but the biting wind pulling at her wet tunic foretold a miserable night unless she found shelter. Her hopes of knocking on a neighbour's door vanished before she reached the first house. There was no smoke from fireplaces or campfires. There were no light sources. No people. No sounds, except for the wind and the waves. Nobody, just burnt-down houses and collapsed stone walls.

Wucestre was dead.

Slowly, Julia passed between the ruins of the largest stone houses along the river. Everything that could burn had burned. The rocks in the walls were soot black; some had cracked in the heat. Burnt iron blades of knives and axes lay among stones and ashes, their wooden handles and shafts consumed by the flames. There were no people, neither living nor dead. Somebody must have returned to bury the dead.

Julia stopped outside the heap of rocks that once was her home. It stood out from the other stone mounds because of the excavated depression in the earth floor. There, she huddled with her brother while the Vikings violated her mother. The floorboards were gone. The trap door was gone. The chairs, table and beds were gone.

Everything was gone.

Daylight was fading, and the chilling wind intensified. This December night would be her last unless she made a fire. Shivering, she walked north between the shore and the forest, where the devastation was less evident. Farthest from the river, a handful of dwellings were abandoned after the Viking raid three years before. The families who lived there were killed or abducted, and the few survivors had moved to live with relatives or find work in the coal mines in Woodhorn.

Their houses were since dismantled by neighbours using the beams and stones to repair their own homes.

Some distance away from the others, Julia found an almost intact building. The fire had reached the wicker roof but was extinguished before it destroyed the walls. The man who used to live there, Heard, was only three or four years older than Marcus. A wooden splinter had taken one of his eyes, and his young wife died in childbirth together with their firstborn. Julia assumed that he was among those who chose death the morning the Northmen went ashore. She mumbled a quiet prayer and entered.

The tiny house was not so different from Cwen's cottage. Heard had dug out the floor hip deep and covered it with branches and planks. The upper part of the walls consisted of stones stacked on top of each other in a ring. Soil and peat sealed the walls. Julia sighed with relief when she found a ragged blanket with singed edges. She would survive this night.

In the forest, she gathered firewood and dry twigs. Back in the shelter, she laid layers upon layers with the thickest wood at the bottom, so that the fire would burn as long as possible during the night. Soon, she was staring into the flames and listening to the waves washing over the sand. Hunger gnawed at her, but she was not cold. In the morning, she would find fresh water in the river. This night, she would sit inside with the flames, safe from the evil and dangers waiting in the darkness outside.

*

With the singed blanket over her shoulders, Julia crossed the bridge to the buildings south of the Wansbeck. Her thin garments fluttered in the wind, much stronger than the night before. The large mound outside the church confirmed her assumptions that somebody had returned to bury the dead. It was a consolation to know that they were laid in consecrated ground. But they were still dead.

Who were they, and who had buried them? Did anyone escape? How many were condemned to a life as a slave, like her mother? Maybe Father and Marcus were lying in the ground underneath her feet, forever lost to her.

Marcus told her about the hut in the marshes and promised to find her again. If he had survived, he would have come for her months ago. He must be dead or enslaved. Father was undoubtedly dead. After what happened to his wife, he would never hide and never surrender.

Her grief was a freezing ache in her stomach that crept mercilessly up through her chest and arms like a snake, rendering her powerless. Tears made her vision blurry, and her courage faded. The short-lived comfort of self-pity washed over her, threatening to drown her.

Julia clenched her fists and pushed back her grief, until all that remained was the discomfort of knowing that the snake of ice was still living in her. One day, it would defeat and devour her. One day, she would be too weak to resist. But not today.

'Rest in peace,' she said softly, turning away.

*

The church was looted and burned, and she found nothing she needed. Julia walked towards the mill, but her hopes of finding unspoiled grain faded with the sound of rats fleeing as she approached. There were a dozen boats by the riverbank; most of them seemed intact. If she managed to pull one of them into the water, she could fish. With what? She searched the vessels for fishing equipment but found nothing of use. Fishermen did not leave their gear in the boats, and everything would have burned up with their homes and storehouses.

Julia crossed the bridge and returned to the ruins of their home. The flames had devoured everything that was not stone or iron. Not a single object, tool or memory remained. Julia climbed down into the excavated cellar that lay exposed under the grey sky. With her back against the earth wall, she cried.

Give up.

Hunger and cold would end her miserable existence before the night was over. It would be even faster if she dived into the river and let the current carry her to the upset sea. The pain would be gone. Never cold, never hungry.

The icy serpent woke up again and swallowed what remained of her hope and courage. Perhaps the snake was the Devil, tempting her to commit the greatest sin of all?

Julia rose. Father and Marcus had not sacrificed their lives for her to drown herself in the river. Determined that she would survive this day as well, she climbed up and left her former home.

At the penultimate house before the quay, she stopped. The walls were reduced to a heap of rocks, blocking her path. Stubbornly, she stepped on the nearest stone and began to balance over the mound. When she put her right foot down for the second time, the stone slid a hand's breadth under her. There was a loud, scraping sound as she slipped. Julia fell forward and scraped her elbow and forearm in the landing. When she got up, she was bleeding from her right knee. Painful, but not a serious injury, she noted. What was that scraping sound?

Julia returned to the stone she had slipped on and lifted it away. Underneath, she saw shining metal. She quickly tossed several rocks away until she could pry out a sword – her father's gladius. Under the stone mound, it lay protected from looters and weather alike.

She could not find the sheath, so her father must have drawn the sword before it was lost. Thus, he had been fighting, and fallen. Even though she had been quite certain her father had died defending the village that fateful morning, it pained her to get the confirmation. Julia turned the sword in her hand as she envisioned him fighting against the invaders, alone against brutish warriors with swords and axes. She imagined Father's facial expression when a heathen thrust a blade into his guts, and the gladius slipped out of a powerless hand. She had pictured it many times before, and it was always like that. He was always alone, and he was always stabbed in his stomach.

'I will return the sword to you, Father!' she said as she rose.

With calm steps, she crossed the bridge a third time, until she once more stood in front of the mound where she presumed her father was buried with the others who fell that morning. Julia knew no suitable prayer for such an occasion. Thus, she climbed to the middle of the mound, grabbed the sword with both hands and drove it into the ground, halfway to the hilt.

Bleeding from wounds on her arms and knees, and with her flimsy clothes fluttering in the wind, she looked around. The village was no more than empty ruins between a cold forest and an angry sea.

With the proper equipment, she could have caught fish. With a bow, she could shoot a deer and have food for weeks. If she had paid more attention when Cwen tried to teach her to set traps, she could have caught hares or birds. In the winter, they lived off what they had collected during the summer and autumn. Julia had nothing and knew nothing that would help her survive her fourteenth winter. Without the goodwill and help from other people, she had no chance.

Father had given his life for her to live. Marcus had probably done the same. She would betray them and their sacrifice if she gave up now.

'I'm going to need this, Father,' she said apologetically, pulling the sword up from the mound again.

'I must go to Woodhorn.'

CHAPTER 22: FORTIFICATIONS

Marcus was already awake when the cold rays of the winter sun lit up the room. Bjarn slept in the other bed. The Northman, the Viking. One of those who had killed his father and abducted his sister. One of the heathens who attacked Irish farms and villages, plundered monasteries and slew defenceless monks who served the Lord. A man whom Marcus had treated for a wound that would kill most people. The Northman, who shared a room with Marcus for many months, willingly taught him his Norse language and trained him to swing the axe with power and precision. An enemy and a friend.

The biting wind howled and whined as it squeezed through the cracks under the roof and next to the frost-covered window. Marcus agonised over spending the whole autumn reading, talking and chopping wood, while his little sister was a prisoner with Torgils. Northmen and Danes had set up two winter camps in Dubh Linn at the Liffey and Linn Duachaill at the Glyde. Come spring, many more would arrive from Lochlann, row their ships up the Irish rivers to plunder, kill and capture slaves. Last year, the Irish had won the battle at Kells. But it had only been a diversionary attack with a few ships. Next spring, the Vikings would come in force, and the Irish clans would be unable to stop them.

The king was dead, they said. Marcus was unsure of the significance, for the Irish had so many kings. The day before, Sechnall visited the convent without talking to Marcus. Abbot

Cearan later told Marcus that Diarmait had deposed his uncle Ruanaid and crowned himself King of Meath. Sechnall was Ruanaid's son, and he responded by killing Diarmait the next day. The usurper was king for one day and one night. King Diarmait was dead. Sechnall mac Ruanaid of the Cholmáin clan was King of Meath.

There was unrest among the other clans in the area. Some supported Sechnall; others did not. Not even within the Cholmáin clan was there peace. Many preferred Diarmait or Sechnall's older brother, Flann. Instead of preparing for war against the invaders, the Irish prepared for war against each other. Clan against clan, and man against man.

Nobody could stop the heathens. Nobody even tried. Nobody dared to fight the great battle, so they all fought the minor skirmishes instead.

Marcus got up and dressed in the warmest clothes he had. He woke Bjarn and advised him to do the same. This morning, they would not attend mass. There were more important matters to attend to, and they had to start now.

Already in the courtyard, Marcus began to see the world with different eyes. The walls surrounding the monastery were neither high nor thick. As they stood, they might slow an attacker, but they would not stop him. Marcus thought about Caesar's writings in Bello Gallico, about how the Romans had built their fortifications against the Gauls. They dug deep trenches and filled them with water or sharpened stakes. They sprinkled the area in front of the palisades with caltrops, jagged pieces of iron that cut open the feet of horses and men who stepped on them. The fortifications were stubbornly defended by legionaries with bows, swords and spears, preventing the enemy from breaching the barriers.

The monastery wall was just a wall.

The abbey could not summon ten thousand men to dig ditches and cut down trees. But during the winter, they could build platforms inside the walls, where Irish archers could stand, provided they found archers willing to refrain from fighting each other for long enough to oppose the Northmen.

Without a word, the pair exited through the gate. The monastery was built on a slight rise, surrounded by cultivated land in all directions. The grounds outside the wall provided little or no protection against arrows, but the Northmen carried large, round shields. To cause any damage, the Irish would need many archers or very skilled archers or fire their arrows from a short range.

Marcus kicked the ground. A thin layer of frozen soil loosened. They would not be able to dig trenches in the ground now. At best, they might be able to do so when the earth thawed in spring, before the Vikings launched their attacks. Ditches were hardly an effective defensive measure against the Northmen who did not attack from horses, as Vercingetorix's Gauls had done at Alesia. It was not possible to dig a trench around the entire circumference of the monastery walls, and an attacking force could just walk around any arbitrary holes in the ground. But if the Irish dug ditches in front of the weaker portions of the walls, they might herd the attackers into areas where the walls were taller, and the archers could hit them with their arrows?

Bjarn looked at him questioningly. Marcus owed him an explanation but was unsure how much to reveal. Bjarn was still a Northman, and the tedious masses hardly made him so enthusiastic about Christ that he would make an effort to defend the monastery. He would gladly follow his countrymen back to Linn Duachaill and resume his life as a raider. There was no reason for him to collaborate on improving the abbey's fortifications.

Bjarn was a warrior from the north, who thought and fought as other warriors from the north. If Marcus could entice him into revealing how he would organise an attack on the monastery, it would be easier to find the countermeasures.

'How many men does Kjetil need to take the monastery?' Marcus asked.

Bjarn raised an eyebrow, and one corner of his mouth pulled up in a knowing smile. He looked from Marcus to the monastery walls and to the surrounding countryside.

'It depends on how many people defend it.'

'A score of monks and novices, and ten Irish archers,' Marcus suggested. He had to start somewhere, without revealing that he envisioned a significantly more substantial defence than that.

'The more men he has, the faster Kjetil wins and the fewer men he loses. Archers are useless in a melee. As soon as Kjetil's men are inside the walls, the battle is over. If he attacks with twenty men, he will probably lose five. Fewer, if the gate is open.'

Bjarn grimaced as if he had chewed on a rotten apple before continuing. 'Kjetil would not waste warriors storming a well-defended monastery. He would pick an easier target, or he would take the monastery by cunning.'

'What kind of cunning?'

'Kjetil is a brutal man. He might threaten to kill some Irish he captures on his way to the monastery. Women and children, perhaps? I can't foresee Kjetil's cruelty, and it will be even worse if Torgils and Aud are involved.'

Marcus was surprised that Bjarn had revealed so much, and at the same time felt something hot and horrible spread through his chest and down into his stomach. He envisioned Aud, smeared in the blood of Irish children, dancing in front of the monastery walls. Who could witness her evil deeds without surrendering to her demands?

The Irish could not win by gathering all their forces in one place and lure the Northmen to attack there. The cunning heathen would never willingly attack a united Irish army. One had to beat them at their own game. Attack them when they were not expecting it and disappear before they could retaliate. Set traps for them. Outsmart them. Defeat them before they reached the monastery.

'Come!' said Marcus and began to walk away from the monastery.

'Where are we going?' Bjarn asked.

'We'll determine the distance from here to the river,' Marcus replied, walking in the direction of the Blackwater.

CHAPTER 23: WINTER CAMP

Ulv crawled out of the mound of skins and furs. Winter was different here than at home. There was frost on the ground, but there was no snow as yet. He fastened the large deerskin cloak around his shoulders and looked over the edge. Below, in front of the cave entrance, Jarl lay staring out into the woods. The dog looked up at Ulv, who said:

'Come on, don't lie there and fret. I haven't slept that long.'

Jarl barked and came rushing up the slope on the side of the knoll. Ulv had found the campsite just a few days after they left Dyflin. A boulder formed a natural lean-to, which Ulv improved with walls made from standing logs, tied together with birch branches and sealed with moss. After several days of hard work, Ulv found that he could not sleep inside the cave. It reminded him too much of a dark, cramped cellar. Thus, Ulv slept under the open sky on top of the boulder, while the cave became a storage area, guarded by Jarl.

That is, Jarl was not a watchdog. The almost adult dog would probably die to protect Ulv, but he showed little passion for defending an area or any objects. Ulv stroked the dog over the tousled fur. 'What are we going to do today, my friend?'

Hunting with Jarl had become truly enjoyable. The forest was full of animals, and Jarl was capable of chasing down game on his own. Mostly smaller animals such as hares and foxes, but lately, he had found the courage to chase larger animals. A deer calf was his latest prey, and the dog was soon a more efficient hunter than his master. Therefore, they had enough meat, skins and furs, but were lacking in other areas.

Ulv had received what he wanted from the warrior outside Dyflin but regretted that he had not asked for a knife that was better suited for skinning and working with leather. Fortunately, he got a whetstone so he could keep the seax sharp. He had foraged some berries before they were spoiled by frost and picked lichen to add to his diet of fried, boiled or dried meat. Ulv never imagined he would miss porridge and gruel.

They were not disturbed by animals or humans. There were people in the area, but Jarl's sharp senses helped the pair keep their distance. The camp was located in a fairly dense forest, making it difficult for anyone to detect the smoke from the campfire, and Ulv was careful not to let the fire be seen. As a rule, he did not light a fire after dark. He was unsure whether he could abide by that rule through the coldest winter nights, but he had managed so far.

Several times they heard wolves nearby, but with so many animals in the forest, Ulv assumed that his namesakes would shun humans.

'Maybe we need more wood before winter sets in?' asked Ulv, looking down at Jarl, who was eagerly gnawing on a bone.

Despite a decent supply of twigs and branches near the camp, they searched farther and farther north until their foraging trip turned into exploration. As Ulv caught the subtle hums of a distant river, he became aware that Jarl was staring in between the trees with ears moving as if trying to locate a sound. The dog was so obedient now that he was rarely leashed. Ulv stalked over to the dog and patted his shaggy coat while he peered in the same direction.

Then, Ulv, too, heard the voices.

Between the trees, there was a glimmer of water, confirming that they were approaching a river. They sat still and waited, but Ulv could neither see the people talking nor hear what they said. He wanted to take Jarl with him and go back to the camp, but something made him curious. More so than usual.

Hunter and dog snuck between the trees, down to the riverbank. Ulv held the bow and two arrows in his left hand. Two men appeared: a short, stocky man and a young man of average stature, both wearing humble garments in brown and grey.

'They will disembark about here,' said the taller of the two men, waving his arms, 'and continue on foot towards the monastery?'

The man spoke decent Norse, but Ulv could hear that it was not his native language. There was something familiar with that voice ...

It was Marcus!

Ulv could not fathom why he did not recognise him at once, but it did not occur to him that the young thrall from Northumbria could walk freely in the Irish wilderness. Ulv arose and walked towards the pair.

The stocky man answered the question. 'Yes, I would think so.'

Both men turned abruptly towards Ulv. The short man's hand went to the axe in his belt, and Ulv recognised him. Jarl barked, and Ulv held up his hands. 'Calm down, Bjarn. It's me, Ulv.'

Both men stared at him.

'Ulv!' exclaimed Marcus. 'What are you doing here?'

'I was going to ask you the same thing,' Ulv said and laughed.

All three were silent for a moment, as if nobody knew where to begin the conversation.

'Let's sit down,' Ulv said, looking around. 'Jarl, you have to guard the area,' he continued, patting the dog. Jarl glared at him and stalked away.

'Jarl?' Bjarn asked.

'Yes,' Ulv replied, grinning.

Bjarn grinned back. 'How inappropriate! Perfect.'

'I thought so, too.'

Marcus smiled impatiently. 'Julia?'

'Sorry, I did not see her in Dyflin. I was not there for long, and much happened during my time there.'

Marcus nodded slowly. They were silent for a moment as they sat down. Bjarn looked from Ulv to Marcus and back to Ulv.

'All right, I have the shortest story, so I can start.'

Ulv and Marcus looked at each other and shrugged.

'Great,' said Bjarn, rubbing his hands. 'Yes, now listen. We were on our way up the Blackwater when an annoying thrall was placed next to me. He could not row, and he prattled like a child.'

'Hey ...,' Marcus interrupted.

'Keep quiet now, monk! Is this my story or yours?' Bjarn replied with a stern expression.

Marcus shook his head.

'Yes, exactly that, a talkative thrall. And that was why I did not notice the archers by the riverbank until it was too late. The arrow struck here,' Bjarn pointed to a spot below his left collarbone. 'And I was stuck to the railing of the boat. Thus, I could do nothing but wait, while the other boys jumped ashore and enjoyed themselves.'

Ulv looked from Bjarn to Marcus. The merchant's son rolled his eyes, but Bjarn kept going. 'As time went by and none of the boys returned to the ship, it struck me that I would be in an unfortunate position if the Irish found me. With painstaking efforts, I tore myself loose from the ship and crawled ashore. Then, I realised the Irish might not be gentle with a wounded Northman. So, I tossed my axe in the river and snapped off the end of the arrow, so that they would not see that I was shot by an Irishman. I had just closed my eyes to take a nap when it dawned on me that I had too beautiful a mane to be taken for an Irishman. So, I drew my knife and cropped my hair over my ears, here.' Bjarn stroked his hands back over his ears.

'Then, it was just a matter of waiting. Boring, but what else can an unfortunate man do when he is pretending to be Irish? The plan worked to perfection. The monks found me and carried me to the monastery. Right up there,' he said, nodding his head in the direction of the abbey.

It was quiet for a moment.

'Yes, that's exactly how it was,' Marcus said, shaking his head. 'Anyway, while Bjarn was lying by the ship, I ran ashore to fight the Irish.'

Marcus gave Bjarn a look as if to emphasise that he had fought in the battle. 'But my first enemy was not Irish. I was on my way through the forest to find the others when a familiar voice roared behind me.'

'Kjetil?' asked Ulv. He knew the answer but was looking forward to hearing the continuation of the unlikely tale the brute had recounted in Dyflin.

'Yes, he pursued me with his sword at the ready. I ran what I could, but he caught up with me. When he was close enough to strike, I had no choice but to throw myself down to the ground, curl up and hope for the best. Luck was with me, for Kjetil tripped over me and slammed into the ground. While he lay dazed, I picked up his sword and ran.'

'But …,' Ulv said, expecting there to be more to the story.

'Yes, it is possible I slipped and put my heel down near Kjetil's nose, or possibly right on it, and stamped down as hard as I might …' Marcus grinned.

Ulv chuckled.

'You never told me that!' replied Bjarn.

'You never asked. Probably because you were too busy pretending to be a wounded Irishman.'

Ulv laughed, and Bjarn and Marcus joined in. Jarl's head appeared between some bushes in the woods. He tilted his head and looked like he was wondering what the three men were doing.

Ulv could not stop grinning. It was good to see Marcus again, and it was good to talk with friends. It had been a long time since he had spoken to anyone but Jarl. And although the dog had proved to be a faithful friend, Ulv missed being part of a group. He pushed back the bittersweet feeling and concentrated on savouring the moment. Right now, at this chance encounter in the woods, he was just going to enjoy the laughter and pleasure of meeting old friends.

'Anyway,' Marcus continued, 'I kept running towards the sounds of battle when somebody called to me again. This time, it was the Jarl. Sigurd sat leaning against a tree with a fatal wound in his stomach. There was not much I could do for him, but I helped him to his feet. With Kjetil's sword in hand, Sigurd spent his moments allowing his men to escape. He challenged a large group of Irishmen and killed several of them before their leader skewered him with a spear. The Jarl suffered a warrior's death, with a sword in his hand and dead enemies around him, saving the lives of his men. The Jarl did not look like a brave fighter, but in the end, he proved he was a true Jarl.'

All were quiet. Bjarn scratched an itch near his eye.

'What happened to you, then?' asked Ulv.

'One of the Irish realised that I knew Latin and brought me to the abbey,' Marcus replied, nodding his head in the direction of the abbey, imitating Bjarn: 'Right up there.'

Ulv smiled and refrained from asking how the Irish discovered that Marcus knew Latin. Instead, he said: 'So you have been there ever since. In the monastery?'

Marcus nodded. 'The abbey of Kells, yes. It is the principal monastery in this area. Relics and valuables from the nearby monasteries are kept there out of reach of the invaders.'

It was quiet for a moment before Marcus asked:

'What about you? What happened in Dyflin?'

Ulv gave his account of the attack and the days that followed until his dispute with Kjetil.

'Suddenly, Kjetil was there, roaring "Wheeelp!" as only he can. Still, I did not recognise his voice right away. It was different, somehow. More nasal.' Ulv smiled. 'He had unmistakably received a heavy blow to his face, and he was not happy about it. He announced that my thrall had attacked him and that it was my responsibility. I said he could discuss the issue with you when he found you.'

Marcus grinned, and Ulv smiled briefly. 'But it was not wise, because Kjetil had predicted my response. He proclaimed that my thrall was my responsibility, and if I could not bring my thrall to justice, I would have to suffer the punishment myself. He was surrounded by his men, and nobody wanted to argue with them. Thus, I was declared an outlaw and expelled from Dyflin.'

Nobody was smiling anymore.

'I'm allowed to return when I've found you, so you can receive your judgement and punishment.'

Marcus snorted. Then all was quiet. The muscles around Marcus's jaw tightened, and his gaze went blank.

Ulv was waiting for Marcus to say something. He did not expect him to volunteer to accompany him back to Dyflin to take the punishment. But he had expected an apology, or at least an admission that his actions had made Ulv's life difficult. A heartfelt plea for release from thraldom? Or even a humble question about what he could do for Ulv in this predicament?

While Ulv pondered all this, Marcus did not utter a word.

Bjarn looked from Ulv to Marcus and back to Ulv again, before he turned his head and shouted: 'What? Yes, of course. I'll come right away!' Then, he rose and strode towards his imaginary acquaintance down by the river.

Ulv wanted to say something but felt Marcus should speak first. Marcus said nothing. His gaze flickered before their eyes met for a moment.

Then Marcus got up. 'Somebody can come looking for us at any time. Then it would be best if you were not here. The Irish are not merciful to Vikings. We … perhaps we'll meet again someday.'

Marcus turned and left. Bjarn caught up with him.

Ulv remained seated until his two former friends disappeared between the trees.

CHAPTER 24: WOODHORN

Julia was frozen to the bone and drained after yet another day without food. She had walked half the day through the woods before seeing the bell tower of the church in Woodhorn. On shaky legs and with her eyes half-closed, she staggered on towards it. She no longer noticed the branches that scratched her skin, and her thin clothes were ragged and stained with blood.

'But, poor girl! What happened to you? Who are you?'

A woman spoke behind her. Julia did not turn to face her but leaned against a tree while uttering the words that kept her alive for the last few days.

'I'm Julia of Wucestre, Gaius's daughter. I'm looking for my brother, Marcus.'

'Julia! Is it really you?'

Julia turned and looked up at the woman. A comforting sense of recognition. The familiar stranger was old, perhaps twenty years older than Father.

The old woman helped her find the answer.

'I'm Esme. Bernia's grandmother.'

'Bernia?' Julia knew nobody by the name of Bernia.

'Abbi. She preferred to be called Abbi.'

Beautiful Abbi, with whom Marcus had been so hopelessly in love. Finally, the pieces fell into place for Julia, and a dozen new questions filled her mind.

'Abbi! Where is she? Where is the rest of your family?'

Esme's face formed a friendly, but sad, smile.

'Come, girl. You need to eat and get warm first.'

The sun was about to set as they walked the last stretch from the forest to the village of Woodhorn. A stone's throw from the church with the tall bell tower, Esme turned left and led her to a cluster of shanties on the outskirts of the village.

The ground was dirty, as if sprinkled with black powder. Fifty paces apart were two pits, like large wells. Above them were racks of wooden poles, and several ropes went down into the holes. A harnessed horse trod in a circle around each of the pits, while a couple of boys walked behind them and slapped them with sticks. Two men emptied buckets of black stones into sturdy carts.

'What is that?' asked Julia.

'Coal,' Esme replied. 'Lord Edric owns almost all of Woodhorn. He digs coal out of the ground and sells it to King Aethelred.'

'Has he become rich from digging coal?' asked Julia. She had never heard of anyone getting rich from hard labour.

'No, Lord Edric has become rich because others mine his coal, which he sells to the king's men. Edric digs nothing himself.'

'What about the miners? Do they get any of the wealth?'

'No. The workers receive two scanty meals at sunrise and noon, and a piece of bread when the workday is over at sunset. And we are allowed to live in these rat nests, as long as we work for the grand lord.'

Esme pulled a leather flap aside and gestured for Julia to enter. The circular shack was not so different from Cwen's earthen hut, but less appealing. Inside were two beds, but no tables or seats. The layers of branches and hay that made up the roof allowed smoke from the fireplace to escape, and wind and rain to enter.

'We don't spend much time here, so it does not matter. We share the beds to keep warm,' Esme said.

'Where are the others?' Julia asked.

Esme sighed, put down her basket and sat on the bed. She motioned for Julia to sit next to her.

'We were a family of eight the morning the heathens attacked: me, my son and his wife, and their five children. My son and eldest grandson took up arms to take part in the defence. Both were slain. The rest of us fled up along the river. At the ford, we were captured and herded back to the beach. The Vikings took Abbi and her mother with them on the ships. They saw no value in me or the three youngest children. Before they left, they set the whole village on fire and left a handful of old people and two dozen children to fend for ourselves without food, equipment or shelter. After burying our dead as best we could without proper tools, we walked to Woodhorn. We arrived at night and were well received with food, warmth and shelter. But after a few weeks, we could no longer live on alms, and we had to find a way to survive.'

Esme put a split log on the fire and draped a blanket over Julia's shoulders before continuing.

'We got by in autumn by gathering food and firewood from the forest, and the families we stayed with benefitted from our efforts. But as the weather got colder, it was challenging to find food, and we became a burden to those who had taken care of us. Therefore, we sought help from Edric. He offered us these houses and three meals a day in exchange for the children working for him. We had no choice. That's why the sons and daughters of Wucestre spend their days crawling on their knees in his dark mines.'

'That's horrible!' exclaimed Julia.

'I don't know how we would otherwise survive. Life is not easy when you have lost everything.'

'Do you also work in the mines?'

'No, I'm too old to crawl around in caves. I gather wood and live on what scarce food I can forage. Lord Edric has allowed me to live here because I have cared for three of the children who worked for him. But now there are only two, and he may oust me when he finds out.'

'Only two? What happened?'

Tears ran down Esme's cheek.

'Our youngest boy, Leof, died of cough a week ago. He had not seen five full winters.'

Julia put her arm around the old woman and let her cry against her shoulder until noises outside made them both get up. On instinct, Julia drew her knife, but lowered her hand when two small figures pushed past the leather flap that served as a door. A girl and a boy, no more than half Julia's age, entered the cramped cabin without noticing her. They collapsed next to each other on the vacant bed. Esme rose and stroked their hair and relieved them of the small straw sacks in their hands. She pulled out a handful of onions and two small pieces of bread and made soup from what the children had earned in the mines.

Julia observed the kids in the light from the fire while the soup boiled. Their wheezing was interrupted by coughing. Coal dust stuck to their clothes and skin. Large holes on their knees and elbows left the skin exposed, and revealed chunks of sand, dust and blood. Even after she washed away the worst of the dirt from their skinny faces, it was hard to recognise them: Mildred and Durwin, Abbi's siblings.

'The soup is warm,' Esme whispered.

Julia sat down next to her in the other bed and was served a wooden bowl with onion soup and a piece of bread. It smelled heavenly, and she ate three spoonfuls in rapid succession and chewed a piece of bread to cool her tongue and palate.

'Aren't you going to wake the kids up so they can eat?' she asked, before she had finished chewing.

Esme looked at her grandchildren.

'They get to eat tomorrow. It's better they sleep as much as possible.'

Julia felt the blush spread on her face. She was gulping down the soup of two small children who had worked in the coal mines from sunrise to sunset.

Embarrassed, she brought her soup bowl and bread and sat down next to the little boy. 'Durwin? It's Julia. Do you remember me?'

The boy opened his eyes and propped up on one arm in bed. Nodding, he reached out to gently touch her face with his free hand. Julia smiled at him.

'Eat some soup before you go to sleep. Tomorrow, I will go with you to the mines, to help you and take care of you.'

CHAPTER 25: PLOY

Geir Galne rambled through the village of Dyflin. The conversation buzzed in his head. His mouth formed words and was still waiting for an answer before he continued the silent dialogue. The muddy ground forced him to jump between the dry parts to avoid getting soaked.

The upcoming conversation was critical to his plan. Geir had to do everything right. No mistakes. No animal stories. Straight to the point, without digressions.

Geir found Olaf inside one of the longhouses in the fortified part of Dyflin. Something had caused Olaf's hair to turn white, but Geir did not waste time pondering it. His focus was sharp as a knife's edge, and as fragile as the ice on a pond after the first night of frost. If Olaf had met another human lately, he would know that his hair had changed colour.

Most people could not keep their mouths shut in such situations, succumbing to the urge to point out what was blatantly obvious: 'Do you know you have a bald spot, Geir?', 'Kjetil, somebody has flattened your nose!' or 'Oi, Stig, you have lost your arm!'

Rarely were such statements helpful or appreciated. A bitter man might answer: 'You don't say? I'm so grateful you told me. I was about to take a bath in the river, and I could have drowned swimming around in a circle without realising the problem. You have saved my life!' Most people would be sad or angered when confronted with stupid comments like that.

Focus, Geir, focus.

The white-haired Olaf stood bent over the long table, a

knife in his hand, studying carved lines, crosses, and runes. Geir examined the patterns in silence, recognising them as a crude map of the islands. He approached the table and pointed at an area on the south-eastern border of Pictland. 'Sigurd Jarl said that the three coastal villages north of Wucestre were too poor for trade or plunder. We ignored them on our route to the settlement at the river's mouth, where the sandy beach offered easy access. Even that place was hardly worth the effort, yielding only a few thralls and handful of silver.'

Olaf glanced up at Geir, down at the table again, and nodded. 'That seems to be the case for the coast of Northumbria.' He pointed with the tip of his knife at the tabletop. 'You would place Wucestre around here?'

Geir nodded, and Olaf carved a cross and a rune. 'And the other villages?'

Geir pointed, and Olaf shaped new symbols.

There was an impressive amount of information carved into the broad planks of the tabletop. Geir had seen such maps before, a useful method of collecting information from everybody you could trust. In this way, they had current knowledge of which towns, villages, ports and monasteries one could visit. And which activities would be most profitable in the different locations. Trade, plunder, thralls, ransom. Or just passing them by.

'And how were their defences?' Olaf asked.

'Pathetic. Peasants with sticks. Untrained and disorganised. Most of them fled at first sight of our sails.'

Olaf made another mark. Geir found a mark he did not understand and put his finger on it. 'What is this?'

'It signifies a person well suited for ransom,' Olaf replied. 'Some of the weaklings, like head monks and priests, are so precious to the churches that they pay us silver to return them unharmed and unspoiled.' Olaf shook his head before pulling up a crooked smile. 'Or at least alive.'

Geir nodded thoughtfully. The scheme was novel to him, but it made sense. He knew the type, and such people made poor thralls. They clung to the distorted belief that the White Christ would intervene and liberate them, so they just sat there with folded hands, mumbling their incomprehensive prayers. Sooner or later, they would give up as the spark of life drowned in a sea of despair.

When Geir met Olaf's gaze, the white-haired man said:

'What brings you here, Geir Galne?'

Geir started the conversation he had performed in his mind thirteen times already: 'I will take responsibility for scouting and coordinating the search for provisions.'

'Is that so? How do you intend to go about improving it?'

Geir had expected the conversation to get to this, but not so soon. Olaf, whose wheel of thought spun fast and accurately, had jumped straight to the heart of the matter. The only reason he would assign this task to Geir was if he knew how to do it better.

Geir had expected Olaf the White to waste time explaining how they customarily handled such matters or ask Geir why he thought he would be suitable for the role. But this direct approach suited him just fine. Geir knew the answer, and he was never a man to stalk around the prey like a cat hunting a sparrow.

'First of all, I would not use ships and rivers. The Irish expect that, and they have moved everything of value to places far off the waterways. Second, I would use horses. If we are not going to use the rivers, we need horses to get around faster. Third, and most importantly, I would encourage trade. Treat the Irish with respect and give them a fair price for their goods. Dispatch a handful of our Irish allies to let the people in neighbouring farms and settlements know that we're open to trade. This way, essential provisions will come to us without sacrificing men in pursuit of it. Fourth, you must instruct our raiding parties always to offer trade as a first option, and only use force if the Irish are unreasonable. But we must always offer better deals to those who willingly approach us to trade. We'll get the provisions we need, without risking our men and provoking our neighbours to attack our camps.'

Olaf looked at Geir with an expression that did not reveal anything. He moved his gaze to the table while flipping the knife into the air and catching it again. Geir opened his mouth to say something but closed it again. He had said what he intended to say. These were the points he prepared. Repeating them would only annoy Olaf. Torgils's trusted advisor did not require things explained twice. A rare breed. Geir ached to keep talking. He opened his mouth to further illustrate his point with the story about the fox, the hare and the leverets, but bit his lip to stay silent.

Olaf tossed the knife in the air again. It spun twice before he grabbed it by the handle. Geir bit his lip until he could sense the salty taste of blood and shifted his weight from one foot to another. And back again. The white-haired man turned to Geir and nodded slowly.

'Valid points,' he said. 'Very well. From today, you are responsible for providing supplies for Dyflin. I will announce the appointment. You report to me every three days.'

Geir nodded, unwilling to risk his fortune by speaking.

'Your reputation is that of a wild dog without a master. Be aware that you are on a short leash now, and I'm your master,' Olaf continued.

'A short leash is fine with me, master Olaf.' Geir flashed one of his rare smiles.

Olaf turned back to the table as Geir walked towards the door. Did Olaf talk about dogs on purpose, or was it a coincidence? One never knew with this man. It was of no consequence: the ploy had worked! Geir got just what he wanted. Now, he was one step closer.

'Geir?' Olaf shouted at him as he reached for the door. Geir stopped and turned.

'You did not inquire about my hair. Why?'

'I figured you knew about that already.'

Olaf nodded, and for the first time since Geir came, he smiled.

CHAPTER 26: DOWNPOUR

Ulv pulled the deerskin over his head and sat listening to the drumming of large drops of water impacting on leaves, rocks and pools. Jarl huddled inside the cave, but Ulv did not indulge in such comforts as a roof over his head. The miserable weather suited his mood perfectly.

His encounter with Marcus and Bjarn had brought him such joy. And sorrow. His delight when he recognised Marcus down by the river was indescribable.

They were not close friends, in the sense that they had a strong bond of affection and loyalty, reinforced by years of shared history. Their connection was different, forged by a few weeks of shared experiences. From the cellar in Wucestre and the voyage to the Norðreyjar, to the struggles with Kjetil Korte. From incomprehensible conversations with Geir Galne, to something resembling support and understanding from Magnus Trygg. They were a team, united in a world of dangers and hostilities. Now, Ulv was alone once more. He envisioned Marcus turning his back on him and walking away.

Maybe he had presented his case in the wrong way. Maybe he should have stressed that Kjetil's ban was a problem they could figure out together. But Marcus seemed indifferent to Ulv's predicament and offered no solution, as if it was all Ulv's fault.

Disappointment turned into anger as Ulv recalled the scene and pondered Marcus's lack of concern and unwillingness to help.

Ulv thought of Father, who did not want his protege to travel abroad. 'The world out there is not for you. You're not a warrior, and you're a poor fit for their way of life.'

Father had prepared Ulv to survive on his own. It was because of this training the adolescent outlaw was still alive. In the forest, he lived comfortably off what he could forage, track and hunt. All because of Father.

Ulv had even held his own in the company of Vikings and fought and killed by their side when they attacked Dyflin. But he also rescued several of the Irish non-combatants, always looking for opportunities to save as many as possible. That was Father's influence there as well. He had been reluctant to teach Ulv how to fight.

Ulv shook his head and closed his eyes.

Tears ran down his cheeks as Ulv limped down the path, but he gritted his teeth and did not allow a single sob to escape from his lips. The last sunrays formed streaks of light through the branches. The air was clear, with a scent of wet soil and blood.

Ulv walked slowly, but still approached too fast. There was the rock from where he always jumped. Yesterday, he had leapt all the way to the large tuft. Such a feat was now impossible. Ulv leaned against the birch and lowered himself from the stone. His body ached, from the kicked leg and the hip that had taken the brunt of the fall, to the stomach and cheeks that had received punch after punch. He could endure the beating and the pain, but he was concerned about the lasting injury to his relationship with Father.

Ulv dreaded Father learning the truth when he got home. His feet subbed along the muddy part of the trail, where he used to hop from rock to rock to keep his shoes dry. There was no hopping this night, and his shoes were already soaked. A salty tear found its way down along his nose, over his lip and into his mouth. He wiped his eyes with the back of his hand. The night was as dark as his mood when he reached the end of his agonising journey. The familiar silhouette in the doorway of the small cabin confirmed that Father was waiting for him, as was his habit when his fosterling was late.

Ulv halted, wondering if Father could see him in the darkness. His feet stopped in the mud under the last trees, unwilling to take another step.

'Ulv?' Father stared straight at him.

Ulv hobbled out into the clearing between the forest and the cabin.

'There you are. It ...' Father paused and stiffened, 'was about time you came home.'

Ulv looked at the ground and made an effort to walk without a limp. Father said nothing until he entered the lighted area in front of the open door.

'What happened?'

'Nothing,' Ulv replied, unthinking. that answer only made it worse.

'Is that so?' Father turned and went inside, leaving the door open. Ulv resolved to answer every question truthfully after that. Father found some pieces of cloth and poured a bowl of heated water from the kettle.

'Close the door.'

Ulv entered and closed the door behind him. Father looked up with a benign expression. 'Come and sit with me, Ulv. Tell me what happened.'

The apprehensive Ulv found his seat on the bench by the table but said nothing. Father dipped one of the bits of cloth in the water, wrapped it around his index finger and began to wipe dirt and blood from Ulv's face.

'What happened, Ulv? Who did this?'

'Nobody. I fell.'

Father raised his eyebrows and gave him a look that asserted he did not have the patience to listen to lies. He sighed as he turned to rinse the cloth in the water. Ulv wiped his eyes behind his back. 'Bjørn. I fought Bjørn.'

'Only Bjørn? Why did you fight?'

'I punched him first …'

Dad turned his head without taking the cloth out of the water. 'Why would you do that?'

'Bjørn said you're not my father, and my birth parents wanted nothing to do with me. That I was so ugly that they left me in the woods to die. Wolves came and sniffed at me, but my stench was so foul that they left me alone. Even the wolves did not want me, not even for a meal.'

Tears flowed down his cheeks again. Father did not speak. The cloth was clean again, and he gently wiped off the blood. His face was sad, remorseful. As if it was all his fault. For a long time, they sat in silence while Father cleaned Ulv's face.

'Do you remember the day you came to me, Ulv?'

Ulv shook his head, not trusting his voice to speak.

'There were troubled times on your father's farm, and there was not enough food to last through the long winter. Your father pleaded with me to take care of you, and I accepted. Very little of what Bjørn said was true, Ulv.'

Ulv nodded.

'I thought you knew all this, but you were just a child. We should have talked about this before. I'm sorry, Ulv. I should not have left you so unprepared for Bjørn's snide remarks, and you should have known more than Bjørn about such matters. Forgive me.'

A tentative smile appeared among the tears on Ulv's face.

'It was as much my fault as yours,' Father said.

Ulv's face flushed with sudden anger: 'It was Bjørn's fault!'

'Yes, he is to blame as well. But there is nothing we can do about him. We cannot ...' Father shook his head and inhaled. 'You cannot control how others behave, what they think or what they say. You can only control how you react. Others may do harmful things to you, but they can never decide how you will react. If you refuse to let Bjørn's cruel words affect you, he will lose his power over you. And you will win. Do you understand?'

'I think so,' Ulv said, nodding.

'It is your responsibility – practice restraint! Master your reactions. No matter what anyone says to you – what anyone does to you – you are in command of your life.' Father sighed and looked down at the table. 'My contribution will be to teach you to fight.'

'Fight?' Ulv repeated the last word incredulously. For years, he had implored Father to commence his weapon training, but he had dismissed it as unnecessary. Had he really changed his mind?

'Yes, fight. You cannot go around getting your face punched in by the likes of Bjørn.'

'But he's much bigger than me and two winters older!'

'Yes, get used to it. This is where the training comes in. Learn to fight against larger and stronger foes. You're slender as a sapling and shorter still, and I don't expect that to change. You've got your strengths; you must develop and use them.'

Ulv looked with astonishment at the man who had been his father for as long as he could remember.

'You're swift as a weasel, Ulv. But you cannot trade blows with anyone. You need to make sure you are not hit and make your own strikes count. We start tomorrow.'

Ulv beamed.

'But one more thing – you should not use the training to take revenge on Bjørn,' Father said.

'Would not dream of it,' Ulv said, grinning.

Ulv opened his eyes without perceiving the water dripping from the branches or the wind rustling through the trees. Instead, he envisioned Father standing slightly bent with a wooden sword in each hand. The very next day, they started combat training – with and without weapons. The exercises always had the same goal: Ulv must avoid getting hit and land some clean strikes himself. His short practice sword was shaped as a seax.

The first weeks were tough, because Father did not pull his punches.

'It's better you suffer some bruises now than a sharp blade to your stomach later.'

Ulv heard the statement a hundred times. Almost every time he was struck, and every time he complained. As his training progressed, Father pushed himself to the limits of his abilities to land his strikes. Months later, he cursed in frustration at not being able to hit the grinning little bastard.

Ulv smiled at the memories. It was after one such day of being particularly annoying, Ulv made his decision. As if he knew what the boy was contemplating.

'Do you remember our agreement about not using your new skills to take revenge on Bjørn?' Father said.

'No, no revenge,' Ulv mumbled.

The next day, the children built a ski jump on the hillside above Gunnar's farm. In addition to Ulv and Bjørn Gunnarsson, there were three other youngsters. Gunnar's brother was visiting and brought his family with him. His daughter, Hildegunn, was Ulv's age, while the two boys were a few years his senior.

Father had fastened a loop to each of their skis, making it possible to jump with them. The invention was not fail-proof, and more often than not, the skis flew in separate directions mid-air. But on occasion, it was possible to land on the skis.

All day, Ulv proved to be the better ski jumper, and Bjørn was not the type to rise above such an insult. His habitual air of superiority melted away faster than the snow below the sun. Ulv's mood, on the other hand, improved with every jump.

At first, he had been cautious. This was the first time he met Bjørn's cousins, and he was concerned about how they would treat him. As it turned out, the teenage boys were friendly and polite, and Hildegunn was a ray of sunshine with a wonderful, contagious laughter. She was also fast on her skis and fearless as she braved the jump that got ever larger throughout the day.

They had just made another expansion to the jump when Bjørn insisted on going first. The others waited at the bottom, ready to mark the distance of what would likely be a new record. Bjørn had already made several spectacular landings and set out to impress his cousins with an awe-inspiring jump. He started his run even higher up the slope than before and kicked off with all his power.

It was folly. As soon as Bjørn left the edge, he waved his arms to adjust the skewed exit. His legs pointed in different directions, and the curved tip of his left ski aimed towards the ground. There was an 'Aaahhh' from Bjørn and an 'Oooiii' from the audience.

Bjørn plunged head-first into the ground, and the skis scattered a dozen paces away. Hildegunn covered her mouth with both hands while all four of them waited for the boy to come up for air. Eventually, a red face emerged from the snow.

'You missed the edge by half a foot, Bjørn,' Ulv said, intended as a friendly piece of advice.

Bjørn was receptive to neither friendliness nor advice. His anger had simmered before his unfortunate last jump, and now he erupted with rage.

'Shut up, you little whelp, or I'll crush your skull.'

Hildegunn and her brothers, who had smiled and chuckled at the whole situation, suddenly fell silent, and the smiles turned to grimaces.

'My apologies. It was just a suggestion.' Ulv said as he slipped the shoes out of the loops. It was evident that Bjørn intended to vent his frustration on him.

'No wonder you're good at skiing, you little shit. Your parents put you out in the woods in the winter to get rid of the feeble dwarf the gods had sent to punish them.'

Ulv struggled to contain his emotions. No matter what Father had said, this was his sore point, and Bjørn knew how to poke at the wound. Clinging to Father's words, Ulv replied:

'My parents had no food. They had to leave me to be raised by others, but they did not leave me to die in the woods.' He despised his parents for abandoning him, yet he felt an urge to defend them and explain.

'Yes, I heard they had to choose between you and an old pig. It was an easy choice, as the hog never did anything wrong.' Bjørn had reached Ulv now and towered above him.

'Stop that!' Ulv said.

'And if I don't? Will you run home to the old man and cry?'

'Stop now, Bjørn, or you will regret your words.'

'You puny bastard! I didn't regret beating you the last time, and I won't regret it now.'

Bjørn pushed Ulv in the chest with both hands. It was not hard, and Ulv merely took a step back to keep his balance. Bjørn, even more irritated, increased his efforts in another shove. Ulv took another step back, but this time he also twisted his body and used his left arm to deflect Bjørn's outstretched arms to the side, forcing him to take a couple of quick steps to stay on his feet. The enraged boy turned and came snarling at Ulv with further intensified efforts.

A fist flew towards Ulv's head, but this time he was ready. The blow missed by a hand's breadth, and once again, Ulv pushed the aggressor away without causing any harm. He sought to give Bjørn the chance to calm down. The outcome was the opposite.

Bjørn flailed like a drunk farmer trying to catch a cat. His broad face was red, and his eyes were mad. His lips were drawn back, baring teeth like a snarling dog.

Ulv realised this fight would not end until one of them was defeated. There was no going back. The memory of limping through the woods, with tears running down his battered face, spurred him on.

A smile spread across his lips.

The next violent blow from Bjørn caught as much air as the first, but Ulv did not push this time. Instead, he evaded the swing and struck with his right fist against Bjørn's ribs, forcing an 'Oooffff!' from his lips.

Perhaps Bjørn should have realised that he was not fighting the same defenceless boy as the previous summer. But he was blinded by rage and wounded pride, and he carried on his futile fight to redeem his honour.

Ulv dodged the wild blows and countered with quick kicks and jabs. The big boy breathed like a drowning sow, but his anger would not allow him to quit. Bjørn roared and rushed forward again, but this time his enemy did not dodge. The three spectators gasped as Ulv stepped forward and extended his right arm, his fist connecting with the head of the charging boy.

Bjørn slumped to the ground.

With an apologetic expression, Ulv looked at his fallen opponent's three cousins and shrugged.

'Go home, Ulv. We will take care of the stubborn pig here,' Hildegunn said in a friendly voice.

'Thank you,' replied Ulv, before he strapped on his skis

and set off for home.

The wind ruffled his hair when he skied down the hill. Despite his hand aching as if he had rammed it into a boulder, Ulv grinned.

'I heard Bjørn got a round of beatings the other day,' Father said at dinner a few days later.

'Mhm …,' mumbled Ulv, staring at his dish.

'How is your wrist?'

Instinctively, Ulv covered his hand and looked up. Father knew, and there was no use pretending.

'I told you not to use what I taught you to take revenge. You don't often do what I say, do you?'

'I … he … it was … it was not revenge, Father.'

'So, you were just defending yourself? Was it not possible to avoid a fight?'

Ulv did not quite know how to respond. It was not his fault. Bjørn had asked for it, even insisted on it. Still, Ulv had longed for that to happen, perhaps even planning for it. And there was Hildegunn. Bjørn was not the only one trying to impress her. Could Ulv have avoided the fight?

'I do not know, Father,' Ulv looked at the table. 'Maybe I could have avoided it. But Bjørn deserved it!' He lifted his gaze to meet Father's.

'I see,' Father said, more worried than stern, 'but you have to listen to what I say, Ulv.'

'Yes, Father.'

CHAPTER 27: HARDBREAD

Geir Galne had implemented his plans immediately upon his appointment. He had dispatched patrols inland, and Irish inhabitants of Dyflin had spread the word about open trade in the surrounding countryside. There was already a score of horses in the newly built stables.

The only thing that did not go according to plan was the trade. None of the locals had taken the chance to come to Dyflin to do business, and one could sympathise with their reluctance.

Still, Geir found no cause for concern. They were not dependent on trade, although it would make things easier. Come winter, with the predictable shortage of food among the war-stricken natives, they might adopt a more practical attitude towards trading with their former enemies.

When they came, it was of utmost importance that they were well received, that they might tell their neighbours about their experiences with the cooperative Northmen in Dyflin. The first few were the key to making it work. Because of this, Geir became very interested when he learned about a single hunter willing to trade a few weeks earlier. By all accounts, he had never entered the town, but if the story was true, it was a step in the right direction. Provided his experience was good, of course.

'Who was the one who traded with the Irish hunter?' Geir asked the man standing with his back to him, brushing one of the recently arriving horses.

'I'm not sure, but I heard it was Hafr,' the man replied

when he recovered from his surprise.

'Hafr Hardbread?' Geir asked, after taking a few moments to recall if there were anyone named Hafr in the camp.

The other man nodded, and Geir headed for the small, round cabins in the western part of town, where most hunters resided. He soon found Hafr among them.

'Are you the merchant?' Geir asked.

Hafr looked at him and opened his mouth, but it was too slow for the impatient berserk. 'Did you trade? With a man? Outside the city?'

'Yes, yes I did. Weeks ago ...'

'Great. Why didn't he enter the village? Who was he? Did you give him an acceptable offer?'

'Yes, he ... Why do you ask?'

'Come on, Hardbread! Answer the question!' Geir hissed.

'Yes, he ... he eh ... I do not know ... eh ... eh ... eh!'

Sometimes it seemed there was nothing at all going in people's heads. Completely silent, empty. Was it any wonder Geir occasionally drew weapons against such people? Not at all, as he judged it. To him, it was quite reasonable to resort to violence when exposed to such hay-brained dwarves. His hand reached for one of the knives in his belt.

'He feared he would not be welcome in town.'

Finally, something sensible rolled out of the food hole of the empty bucket that was Hafr Hardbread.

'Didn't you tell him we were open to trade, and offer him profitable terms?'

'Profit ...?'

'DID YOU TELL HIM HE WOULD GET GOOD TERMS WHEN TRADING WITH US?' Geir had taken a step forward, and his words splattered over the unfortunate Hafr. He did not intend to spray him in spittle. It was just so difficult to interact with such hens.

Hardbread retreated a few steps. 'I ... yes, I told him ...'

Geir stared at Hafr and made a cranking motion with his hand, as if that might make him think faster.

'I said so. I told him the city was open for trade.'

Geir had to bite his lip not to strike him down on the spot. Now, he cranked with both hands in front of Hafr. Even Geir was surprised to notice he held a knife in one hand.

'I told him to take his furs to trade in the town. But he wouldn't risk encountering Flatnose. I mean Korte. Kjetil Korte.'

Geir could not care less if Hardbread referred to the newly appointed Jarl of Linn Duachaill as Flatnose, Korte or Dungheap, as long as he got to the point before Geir died of old age. 'Why was this man afraid of Kjetil?'

'He did not want to meet Kjetil, as he was the one who had forced him to leave Dyflin.'

'What do you mean? Was he one of Kjetil's men? Speak, dimwit!'

'Eh, no, it was the youngster Kjetil outlawed last autumn.'

Geir drove his fist into the repulsive snout of the empty head attached to his body in front of him.

It was Ulv, right outside Dyflin!

The wheels spun in his head. Geir closed his eyes, turned, and began to walk. After a few paces, he opened one eye a little so he could see where he was going. With which hand did he strike Hafr? The empty hand, or the one with the knife?

He could have learned more from the hollow barrel of a man. After all the empty noise, he spilt the valuable sounds towards the end. Hafr might know more, even something important. Was it too late? Was Hafr dead?

With his open eye, Geir glanced down at his knife. It was clean, with no blood and none of the gore that was inside heads. Would the knife be clean if the man's head was empty? Geir turned and saw Hafr kneeling with his head in his hands, still alive. He had more luck than he deserved.

Geir sat with closed eyes and his back against a wall, listening to his breath gradually calming down. The wheels in his head had also stopped or slowed down enough to be overlooked. He no longer felt the urge to kill anyone, at least as long as he did not have to speak with anyone. The sounds from the river were no longer deafening, and the stench of rotten vegetables, mud and smoke was not as repugnant as before. Exhale, inhale. Ulv had been there, just outside the town. Trading.

It should be possible to obtain more information, even from an empty skull. Where had Ulv come from? What was he offering, and what did he need? Where did he go? Geir considered interrogating Hafr Hardbread again but discarded the notion. It wouldn't work, and Hafr would probably lose his head before Geir got anything sensible out of him.

Was Vass in the town?

Geir got up and found the Dane in the longhouse that was open to the commoners. Dyflin was crowded during winter, and there was no room for everybody in Torgils's hall. Geir had suggested they open one of the longhouses to all the warriors who had no other place. Olaf then decided that every man had to pay for his beer with hacksilver or any other trinket or item of value.

Olaf had found the right man to keep track of it all. Gorm Skalle remembered everything he had ever seen or heard. At least that was his reputation. Thus, Gorm was given the task of keeping track of how much beer each of the guests in the beer hall could drink until they had to come up with more goods or silver. This practice came with several benefits. First, the longhouse was no longer crowded, and second, Torgils profited from it all.

Geir was not surprised to find Vass drowning his

boredom in the bottom of a beer mug in the smoky longhouse. He would have to remedy that. But first, he would use the Dane to solve his own problems.

'Vass!'

The young wolfskin looked up and smiled. 'Geir! Are you thirsty?'

'No, and surely you can't be either. I need your help. Do you know Hafr Hardbread? Can you go and talk to him?'

'Sure. Tomorrow,' Vass replied, lifting the mug as an explanation. His thick voice revealed that it was not his first mug of beer.

Geir knocked the mug out of his hands. Vass's gaze suddenly became clearer, more focused.

'Now?'

'Yes, now! Hafr has spoken to Ulv, recently. I need to know everything he knows about our young friend.'

'Ulv? Here? All right, I'll talk to Hafr.' Vass put his hands on the table to get up but stopped halfway. 'Why don't you talk to him yourself?'

'I tried,' Geir replied.

'I see,' Vass said, and headed for the door. Geir noticed that the wolfskin did not ask why he was so interested in Ulv but pushed the thought away. It was not important.

The storm in Geir's head abated. Vass would uncover all that was to know about Ulv. The Dane had one of the calmest minds he had ever encountered. His wheel turned steadily, without ever getting out of control or stopping. Stable and reliable, driven by a broad and calm river with crystal clear water. No matter what Vass was doing, his wheel spun at a pace that was perfectly suited to the task at hand.

Provided there were tasks for him to attend to.

CHAPTER 28: COUNCIL

The council was not going well.

Marcus glanced at the thirty men in the room. He knew only three of them. At dawn, Sechnall mac Ruanaid, the new King of Meath, and his brother Flann had come for abbot Cearan and Marcus in Kells. The others were prominent Irish farmers from the area around the Boyne and Blackwater rivers. Half a dozen of them had their farms near the Northmen's winter camp in Linn Duachaill, and they had been richly rewarded for providing food, tools and horses for the finngaill during winter. Some Irish even allied themselves with the invaders and seized the grazing areas of plundered neighbouring farms.

The farmers listened as the king spoke of their honour and duty to Ireland, but their frowns and crossed arms indicated that his words did not move them. Some looked at the ground or shook their heads as their king urged them to prepare for war against the Vikings.

The farmers were running out of patience, and a handful of them got up from the benches and headed for the exit.

'You will burn!' Marcus exclaimed in a clear voice.

His mastery of spoken Celtic was not yet good enough for a normal conversation. Even if he often knew the right words, he used them wrong, so the meaning came out different from what he intended. Now, he had plenty of time to consider this very sentence and made the mistake on purpose.

The departing Irishmen stopped and looked at the young monk who had threatened them. Their faces revealed a mixture of anger and confusion. Some reached for their swords, finding nothing but an empty sheath. The king held the council in a church just north of where the river An Abhainn Dubh, or Blackwater, flowed into Boyne. Nobody was allowed to carry weapons in a church.

'You will burn,' Marcus repeated.

Marcus knew the Irish could perceive his words as a threat, an insult or even a curse. The statement had had the effect he wanted: he had their full attention. Before he could continue, before he could persuade them, he had to calm their minds.

'Vos can transferendum quid dicam?' Marcus turned to Cearan, who was fluent in both Latin and Celtic. The abbot confirmed with a hesitant nod.

Marcus's body trembled. He was alive and doing something important. He covered a nervous yawn behind a clenched fist and positioned himself in front of the altar, visible to everybody. Cearan stood by his side and translated.

'The foreigners come with swords and fire. In one day, ten days or a hundred days. They will come before dawn, and fearful screams will awake you. From your child or a servant looking for firewood. There is no time for you to get dressed, but you grab an axe and run out into the yard to meet them.'

Marcus paused to let Cearan translate into Celtic. He kept his eyes on a sturdy Irishman with his arms crossed over his chest as he continued.

'The Northmen are superior warriors, whether they fight alone or together. They will slaughter you like sheep.'

He shifted his gaze to a young man, whom he assumed to have a young wife and children.

'The fortunate among you will live to witness the heathens defiling your wives before your eyes. The savages laugh when your women cry, and they laugh even more when you try to break free to help them. If you struggle too hard for their liking, they will slit your throat or thrust a sword in your stomach.'

Marcus paced the floor slowly, looking from man to man, until Cearan was silent again. He lowered his voice when he continued.

'When they are finished with your wives, they turn to your daughters. Or sons, if they prefer. Those who survive are taken as slaves.'

Every eye was looking at Marcus. He had struck their hearts and made the threat evident to them. Pained expressions revealed that they envisioned the events.

'When their appetites are satisfied, they go from house to house and loot everything they need: food, leather, tools and silver. Before they leave, they set every building on fire. You can live off the land for a few months, but come winter, you must beg for food and shelter.'

The silence that followed told Marcus that the first task was accomplished.

He poured himself a mug of wine while waiting for the inevitable resistance from men seeking to avoid dealing with an unpleasant truth.

'Bah!' exclaimed one of the farmers. 'We trade with the finngaill. They need us!'

Marcus drank a few sips of the wine while waiting for Cearan's whispered translation and the predictable response from the others in the room. Several nodded approvingly and voiced their support. Men would do anything to avoid discomfort, even cling to a blatant lie. Calmly, Marcus put down his mug and addressed the man who led the opposition.

'Do they?' Marcus asked.

'Sure! I have hundreds of cattle, and the Northmen need meat, milk, cheese and wool!' said the confident Irishman.

'They need your cattle, yes. But do they need you?'

'Without me, they don't get my cattle!' the farmer replied.

'You do not own the animals. The Northmen let you shepherd them until they need them.'

Marcus looked the man in the eye. He spoke slowly, allowing Cearan to translate each sentence at a time.

'The Northmen are getting stronger every week. Soon, their ships will arrive with supplies and more warriors from Lochlann. In spring, the fair strangers will offer half the price for your sheep. In summer, Kjetil Jarl and his men come to the farm and demand to buy your wife as well. If you give in, you are a man without honour. If you refuse, he will kill you and give the farm and your wife to one of his housecarls.'

The Irishmen mumbled and seemed angry, but nobody opposed Marcus.

'Savages. Cowardly rats!' exclaimed one of the farmers.

Marcus laughed, as he knew he would get more attention if he surprised his audience. Thirty pairs of eyes were on him.

'Cowards? No! The Northmen are not cowards. They possess great courage and great strength. Vikings can take your farms, your animals, your women and children, your honour and your lives. Because you permit them to do it.'

'What do you mean?' This time it was the king who spoke.

'A man without the strength and courage to defend himself is worthless in their eyes. Instead of fighting against them, you call the heathens neighbours and allies and cling to the hope that they will not harm you. As sickly animals are prey to predators, weak Irishmen are prey to the Northmen.'

All resistance died. The truth washed away the lies as the tide washes away the sand. Men without hope are a sad sight. Marcus sympathised with their discomfort. He waited in the knowledge that each man was searching for a new hope.

'We can attack their winter camp before they get

reinforcements,' suggested one.

Their eyes were on Marcus. He had taken away their hope, and they looked to him to give it back to them.

Marcus kept calm. The Irish needed a strong leader in the war that would come. An escaped thrall, a young lay brother from a foreign land, could not unite the clans.

'Behind the palisade, every Northman is worth ten of us,' Sechnall replied.

Marcus nodded. The king rose to the occasion.

'We must lure them out and face them on the battlefield!' suggested another.

Marcus met Sechnall's gaze and shook his head slightly.

'Brother Marcus of Northumbria. You have fought the Northmen in many battles, and you know their ways. Will it work?' asked the king.

Marcus coughed in his hand to conceal a smile when Cearan translated the question from Celtic to Latin. Sechnall mastered Latin himself and did not require the abbot's assistance. Their conversation was adapted to capture the hearts of the Irish farmers; thus, the king's description of Marcus was far more flattering than deserved. The merchant's son accepted the role as the king's advisor.

'My King,' replied Marcus, 'you are right, of course. You can't attack the heathens in their fortified camp. You will suffer great losses before you get the first man inside the palisades, and there he will encounter enemies who are far beyond his skills at arms. The king speaks wisely.'

'Neither can you engage them in open battle,' he continued. 'The Northmen have fought many battles, and they learn from both victories and defeats. You would need three or four warriors to every one of theirs to win the day. If you managed to convince that many of your brethren to take up arms, Kjetil Jarl would not face you on the battlefield.'

'Exactly!' said Sechnall, as if Marcus had only confirmed what was already evident to the king. 'We must be prepared to harass the Northmen in small groups when they leave their fortified camp.'

'How do we know when they leave camp?' asked Flann.

Sechnall smiled and pointed to Marcus while he poured more wine for himself, as if everything were thought through and decided between them beforehand. Everybody looked at Marcus, again.

'We provide them with an opportunity they can't resist,' said Marcus.

'How?' asked the king, still with a friendly and calm expression, as if he already knew the answer.

'The Northmen were routed at Kells last autumn. King Sechnall slew their Jarl. Their sense of honour compels them to avenge their defeat and prove worthy of fighting side by side with their pagan gods. If we tempt them to attack at a particular location, we can decide where to fight them.'

'And which location would you sacrifice to this end?' asked Cearan. His expression revealed that he knew the answer.

'The abbey of Kells,' Marcus replied in Celtic.

'We cannot defend a monastery against an army of savages!' Cearan was not happy with the plan.

'We will entice the Northmen to attack the abbey of Kells, but that is not where our forces will engage them. To bring their army to Kells, they must row their ships from morning to night up the rivers Boyne and Blackwater, which you call An Abhainn Dubh. Thus, we know where they come, and we can attack them in small bands of warriors and archers at advantageous points along the river.'

'But how do we know when they come?' asked one of the farmers.

'We cannot know for sure. Therefore, we must make sure

to alert all the farms when the day comes. I suggest you build a beacon overlooking the Boyne where she flows into the sea and put a guard there. When the Viking ships appear on the river, the guard lights the beacon. The Irish will see fire and the smoke and know that the day has come. Each large farmstead contributes with five or ten men and women armed with bows, spears and axes. These small bands cut down trees to create obstacles in the river and attack the ships with arrows. When the Northmen disembark to engage them, the Irish bands retreat into the forest and regroup further upstream. This way, the Irish forces will become more and more numerous further up the river, and all can unite in defence of the monastery at Kells before nightfall.'

'Do you suggest our women join the battle against the Northmen?' asked Flann.

'If their men lose the battle, the women will suffer. Men show more bravery when they fight with women by their side. And the arrow from a woman's bow is as deadly as the arrow from a man's bow,' Marcus replied.

The Irishmen were silent. Some nodded, nobody objected. After a while, King Sechnall concluded:

'So be it. We prepare for war.'

CHAPTER 29: BEER

Ulv went through his seax routines. In the absence of a sparring partner, he had begun practising combinations of thrusts and cuts without opposition. He started with a simple drill with a low slash, a high stab and then a sweeping blow. After a few rounds of this, Ulv got bored and had started to expand by evading imaginary blows, dodging arrows and twisting away from spear thrusts.

After a while, the routine had become so long that he did not want to expand it further. Instead, he worked on making the movements more accurate. To achieve the desired precision, he slowed down his moves. This proved to be taxing, so Ulv alternated between fast and deliberate combinations. If nothing else, he improved his endurance by doing the exercises slowly. But he discovered another effect as well. The fast manoeuvres felt better and more precise after he had executed them slowly hundreds of times. Also, the monotonous repetitions calmed his mind and improved his mood.

Ulv sat and took a sip of water. He was warm and happy. Jarl lay with his head on his forelegs and looked at him.

'Are you bored? Shall we go for a walk?' asked Ulv. The wolfhound turned lazily on his head and looked to the side. Ulv mimicked his companion's move, and his heart skipped a few beats.

Geir Galne stood in the middle of his camp.

The tall, slender man looked around with an inquisitive stare. A straw dipped in the corner of his mouth. He put down the sack he carried over his shoulder and scratched Jarl's neck.

'Where's your thrall?'

Straight to the point and without mentioning a single animal. Ulv was not sure if that was a good or a bad sign, nor did he know how to answer. Lying to the volatile berserk could be fatal. Making him wait for an answer was hardly a safer approach. Fortunately, Geir's impatience broke the tension.

'You know you can come back if you bring him with you?' Geir looked around and gestured at the camp. 'This is not a life worthy of a young Northman. You don't owe that thrall anything, boy. You were finally accepted, and he stole your life and future by attacking Kjetil. Besides, Flatnose is no longer in Dyflin. Everything will be as they be, and you can even keep your thrall. You can get your life back.'

Ulv had to say something. His hands were clammy, and his heart was still pounding. Even though Galne seemed calm enough, he could boil over with anger any moment.

'How do you know he's alive?' asked Ulv.

'I don't know for certain, but he was not found among the dead,' said Geir.

'Why did you come here to tell me now? Why does my predicament matter to you?'

Galne's eyes narrowed, and his nostrils widened. Ulv's hand found the hilt of the seax in his belt. A moment passed. Then another. It was completely quiet until Jarl growled softly.

Geir Galne inhaled and released the air through his nose. His face relaxed, the straw in the corner of his mouth shifted as a smile reached his lips. 'I thought you would share what you know with me, as I share what I know with you. You know, a cow for a barrel of beer? If your thrall is still alive, he was probably captured by the Irish. And if he is held captive, he is likely to be kept in their headquarters.'

Ulv nodded thoughtfully, and Galne continued:

'Do you know where he is?' The impatience was back in

his voice.

'Yes.'

Galne made signs that he should continue.

'Yes. I've seen Marcus. And Bjarn.' Ulv expected a reaction, but Galne only made a circling motion with his hand, urging him to continue.

'They're both in the monastery not far from here. Kells, I think he called it.'

'Good. Do you know anything else?'

'They also said that the Irish had collected valuables from the surrounding monasteries and churches in Kells and believed that was a place they should be able to defend.'

'Is that so?'

'Yes, that's what they told me, anyway.'

Geir Galne grimaced as he pondered the implications. 'They will get what they wish for, then. We will attack their monastery in spring. Find me if you want to join us, and I'll find a place for you. This raid will surely please the Æsir.'

Ulv nodded.

'I brought this.' Geir handed the sack to Ulv. 'And if you need to trade your furs, just come to Dyflin. Ask for me if you need anything.'

Galne got up and left the camp.

Ulv remained deep in thought. For the first time, he saw an opportunity to restore his position among the Northmen in Dyflin. Had he sentenced Marcus to death with his revelation? No, there must be a way to solve several problems at once. He could help the Northmen and save Marcus and bring him back to Dyflin. Together, they could find Julia and fulfil Ulv's promise.

It was the kind of deal Loke would have made. He was playing both sides, betting everything on the belief that he could make it work somehow.

Ulv had heard some of the Northman comparing his luck

and trickery with that of Loke. Maybe they were not entirely wrong. Ulv had not given much thought to appeasing the gods lately. Perhaps he should do something about that and make a sacrifice the next time he brought home prey from hunting. He would need some luck and goodwill in the weeks to come. It could not hurt.

In the spring, Ulv would take part in the attack on the monastery. It felt good to have a purpose beyond staying alive.

Ulv opened the sack and found two small bags of grain, two wedges of cheese, a piece of dried fish and a small keg of beer. It had been a long time since he had drunk anything but water.

A smile spread across the face of the young, outlawed Northman.

CHAPTER 30: AMBUSH

Vass had woken up when Geir Galne ripped the blanket off him, barked a series of commands and left before the Dane had the time to get out of bed. Vass got dressed, splashed cold water on his face and grabbed his equipment before he stumbled out of the small house. Better get to work sooner rather than later when Galne was in that mood.

Soon, Vass left through the west gate, accompanied by ten berserks. The day before, Galne had informed them that they would sail to Linn Duachaill on the first day of spring. Kjetil Flatnose, who was now Kjetil Jarl, had requested reinforcements for a planned attack on the abbey of Kells. Torgils, or more precisely, Olaf, had decided that Geir Galne and his band of berserks were well suited for the task.

The band followed the River Liffey on foot and turned north towards the monastery in Kells. Vass's men were seasoned warriors, fully capable of keeping quiet and following orders. The first day was uneventful, and by noon the second day, the scouting party reached the Blackwater and followed the south bank west towards Kells. If the Irish planned anything in this area, the berserks would soon learn about it.

Despite the apparent tranquillity, trepidation grew among the members of Vass's band. They trod carefully, their heads turned more often, and they communicated only by hand signals and the occasional whisper. The ground and undergrowth were wet, and large snowflakes fell from above and melted on their clothes and skin.

Vass sent two men to scout ahead of the group, while one followed a bowshot behind them.

As they approached a clearing in the woods, Vass raised his hand and pulled off his hood. His men spread out around him and crouched to stay out of sight. They had passed through dense vegetation, and open areas like this were few and far between. The Blackwater was barely visible thirty paces to their right.

'Why do we stop?' Gunnar whispered. Water dripped from his balding head, and there was a hint of irritation in his voice.

'Something is wrong,' Vass replied, surveying his surroundings.

'Yes, it's wet and cold, and we are on a meaningless ...,' Gunnar hissed, before he was interrupted by a chorus of 'Hush!'

Gunnar fell silent. And with that, the soft rumbling from the river was all they heard.

'They should have been back,' Vass said, looking up at the sky. The sun hid behind a dense layer of clouds.

His two advanced scouts had returned at regular intervals, but now they had been gone for a long time. Vass pulled his wet hair back and looked behind. The snowflakes melted as they reached the muddy ground, but their tracks were deep and easy to follow. How long had it been since they had seen Kolbein, the rearguard?

'Stein? Do you see any other tracks here?' Vass looked down at the ground.

Stein was already examining the ground in front of them. He held a bow and an arrow in his right hand while he moved around like a two-legged tracking dog. Some of the others joined him in the search while Vass peered into the forest in front of them.

‘There is somebody waiting for us there,’ Vass whispered.

‘I find no tracks but our own,’ said Stein, ‘but an enemy would stay in the woods rather than expose himself in open terrain.’

‘You see ghosts in broad daylight!’ snorted Gunnar. ‘I’ll go get them.’ The warrior clenched his axe stalked into the forest in front of them.

Vass considered stopping him, but hesitated. Maybe Gunnar was right, and the two scouts were nearby. Besides, if they did not return, somebody would have to look for them anyway. He might as well send somebody who volunteered. While Vass pondered this, Gunnar disappeared into the bushes. For a while, they heard the sounds of bending branches and cracking twigs. Soon, only the river’s song could be heard.

Vass drew his sword and axe. ‘Half circle! Backs to the river.’

The berserks drew weapons and shields and fell in formation. Vass’s heart pounded as he looked for enemies in between the trees and bushes.

‘Aaargh!’ The outcry came from the direction where Gunnar had disappeared a few moments earlier. Immediately, two of his companions rushed towards the sound.

Vass stopped them. ‘Wait! We can’t charge blindly into the forest. That’s what they want. Stay together. Two rows, three steps apart.’

The column advanced slowly towards the forest edge, when Vass saw movement. It was Gunnar. He returned, but he was staggering and clutched both hands to his neck. There was blood, lots of it, seeping out between his fingers and down his arms. His mouth opened, but there was no sound. Stein and Arild rushed forward.

‘Stop!’ Vass commanded, to no avail.

Gunnar sank to his knees and toppled over. Stein arrived

first and bent over his prone companion. Ten paces behind him, Arild screamed as he was pulled to the side. Moments later, his legs protruded from a thicket. To his right, no more than ten paces away, Vass spotted a figure dressed in brown and green garments. He turned and looked at Vass with intense eyes in a black painted face. Then, he jumped over a rock, rolled between some ferns and disappeared.

Vass briefly considered charging after him but decided that he would be at a severe disadvantage confronting one or more unseen enemies in unfamiliar terrain.

Gunnar and Arild lay lifeless in pools of their own blood. Vass reckoned that his three scouts were similarly executed. Of the ten berserks who followed Vass out of Dyflin, only half remained.

'Get out in the open. Now!'

Vass retreated towards the clearing while his eyes searched the woods around him. The six berserks pulled the two bodies with them and reassumed the semicircular formation with their backs to the river. 'Well, men, we have our answer. The Irish are keeping a watch on the Blackwater. We must return to Dyflin and report.'

'What do we do with our dead?' Stein nodded to their slain companions.

'We leave them here. Take their equipment. Leave nothing for the Irish.'

Several of the men mumbled with dissatisfaction. Vass continued: 'Our brothers are dead, but we are still alive. I will not lose more of you. Sometimes, we have to leave fallen friends on the battlefield. So too today. Stein, lead us. I cover the rear.'

Soon, the band of berserks left the clearing and commenced their slow and perilous march towards Dyflin. A farthing east of the clearing, Stein halted. The others also stopped, and all looked ahead. In front of them stood a pole, decorated with a disembodied head. A familiar head, despite the contorted expression.

'Kolbein,' Stein said, and approached the pole.

Kolbein was the scout Vass had instructed to stay some distance behind the others. Vass shifted his gaze from the dead, staring eyes to the surrounding forest. Inside, his anger glowed like burning coal.

A rustling sound made Vass shift his gaze to the right. The slight movement of a branch was enough for Vass to spring into action, and a moment later, a figure jumped up from a bush and darted between the trees with the enraged Vass in heedless pursuit. Shrubs and branches rushed past and scratched his face and hands. Despite his best efforts, Vass could not keep up the pace in rough terrain and frequent changes of direction, and he eventually lost sight of the enemy.

Still, Vass kept running in the direction of the last sighting of his elusive foe but slowed down when he spotted footprints in the soft ground, leading to a rock encircled by dense fern. The wolfskin held his axe in one hand, and now he also drew his sword.

Vass approached the stone cautiously. His gaze was fixed on the ferns, but he did not expect to find the enemy there. Neither did Vass have any hope of surprising the Irish predator, but the less noise he made, the more he could hear. Behind him, some of his men were shouting his name. Vass gripped his weapons tightly. Almost there. One more step.

Vass spun around and swung his axe in a wide arc. The man behind him jumped away, and the axe blade sliced a wide gash across the belly of the woollen shirt. The berserk pressed on, chopping from above with the sword and swinging the axe in another arc, but the enemy backstepped and evaded. His skin was smeared brown and black, and in his right hand was a long knife with a bone handle.

Confident that the slippery ground put a retreating opponent at a disadvantage, Vass advanced and stabbed with his sword – an attack that would pierce the enemy if he repeated his previous defensive manoeuvre. The Irishman did not retreat, however. Instead, he sidestepped, leaving Vass's left flank vulnerable to a deadly counterattack.

Vass knew he was in trouble and needed to get as far away as possible from the blade that had already slain five of his companions. Rolling to his right, he twisted his body and swung his axe upwards in a desperate attempt at parrying. There was a loud clang when the knife struck the axe head.

The Dane landed in a sideways roll, anticipating the sharp pain of a knife blade between his ribs. The decisive thrust never came. When Vass got to his feet, Stein appeared from behind a tree, and the Irishman was nowhere to be seen.

Vass turned slowly with his weapons at the ready, his eyes and ears searching for any indication of his enemy's presence. There was neither movement nor sound, except for the noises of the approaching band of berserks. Vass lowered his weapons as his men came into view, breathing heavily.

Stein looked at Vass. 'Are you wounded?'

'Not yet,' Vass replied, annoyed.

'Who was it? Were they many?'

'Only one. Finn.'

'Finn?'

'One of the Irish who escaped our attack on Dyflin. He's dangerous and has every reason to hate us.'

Stein and the others looked at Vass in bewilderment.

'We slaughtered his whole family that day. Aud sentenced his little sister to die after the battle was over.' Vass shook his head.

*

'What did you learn?' Geir Galne asked before Vass had come through the door.

The chieftain lay on his back on a bench in front of the

fireplace in his small house. His eyes were closed, and his hands folded behind his head. 'Are the Irish preparing for an attack?'

'They are keeping a close watch of the area, and you can safely assume they are preparing for war.' Vass sat down on the vacant bench on the other side of the fire and stretched his hands out towards the heat.

Galne turned his head and opened one eye to look at Vass.

'I lost five men, Geir.'

Geir Galne sat up, his bulging eyes wide open. 'Ambush? Were they many? How close came ...'

Vass looked up from the flames and gave the experienced berserk a look so stern that Galne stopped talking. Instead, he bit his lower lip, got up and started walking a few steps back and forth.

Vass stared at the flames again. 'It was Finn,' he said in a low voice.

Galne stopped pacing and looked at Vass, who answered before the question was uttered:

'Alone. First, Finn eliminated my scouts. One at the rear and two in front. Nobody noticed until too much time had passed without them returning. At a clearing in the dense forest, we stopped to investigate the situation. Gunnar grew impatient and decided to go searching for them, alone. I let him go ...'

Vass fell quiet, and Geir resumed his pacing.

Moments later, the Dane cleared his voice and finished his report.

'Gunnar returned, with his throat slashed open. He was dead before we reached him. Even there, in our midst, Arild was captured and killed. We could not see the enemy, just his victims. With five men departed for Valhall, we set course for home.'

Once more, it was quiet in the small house before Vass continued:

'We found Kolbein's head on a stake. That was when I sensed an opportunity to catch him. I figured he would attack again when we stared at Kolbein's severed head. Finn allowed me a glimpse of him, and I pursued him into the woods. As expected, I lost track of him, and he circled behind me. I waited for him to strike, and I almost got him. I got the upper hand but pressed my advantage too far, and he almost rewarded me with a knife between my ribs. Finn disappeared when my men arrived.'

'And you are certain it was Finn? And that he was alone?'

'Yes. I've seen him before. I remember those eyes. And this was personal.'

'What do you mean?' asked Galne.

'He could safely attack us with his bow, but he prefers the knife. Up close, with blood on his hands.'

'He didn't want to be seen, perhaps?'

'Yes, but even after we knew he was there, he used the knife. He's simmering with hatred, yet he is cold as ice. He is dangerous. Ruthless.'

Galne nodded slowly but said nothing.

'The way he sent Gunnar back to us with a slashed throat. How he used Kolbein's head to unsettle us ...' Vass shook his head.

Geir Galne put his hand on the younger warrior's shoulder and squeezed.

'We should stay away from that river.'

CHAPTER 31: GOODBYE

Ulv stirred the porridge he had made from the grain Geir Galne gifted him. The scent brought memories of happier days back home, before he had the childish notion of proving his worth to Sigurd Jarl. Ulv had visited the farm of Hundolf, Jarl of Gaular, Sigurd's rival. There, he stole Hundolf's ornate silver goblet.

By presenting the goblet to Sigurd, Ulv intended to demonstrate that he possessed qualities the Jarl needed. Sigurd, on the other hand, was not impressed and declared that he only needed warriors. Thus, Ulv was given the dubious opportunity to redeem himself by proving his worth as a warrior on a Viking raid. It had all gone downhill from there, leading to his current predicament as an outlaw in the wilderness of a hostile land.

But his visit to Hundolf's farm brought something good with it. While hiding inside the longhouse, Ulv met the woman with the most gorgeous eyes. She looked at him without fear and helped him escape. Ulv often thought of her. Her long dark hair and fair skin, the red lips that hinted at a smile. And those dark eyes. She was older than him, perhaps by ten or fifteen winters.

Ulv shook his head and sighed. Dreaming of the past did not make his life easier, but there wasn't much else for him to do. The visit to Gaular Jarl's farm had not been how it all started, anyway. That was the day he decided to say goodbye and leave home.

Ulv stood at the door, ready to leave. Father had sat in

silence and watched him pack. ‘Ulv, you do not belong in their world. I did not raise you to think like them. They have so many rules and customs that do not suit you.’

‘I have made up my mind, Father. I don’t want to sit here all my life. You have taught me so much, and I’m sure I will find a way to fit in.’

Ulv tried to smile but did not quite make it. He could not stand disappointing Father and was on the brink of cancelling his plans and staying home. He had disobeyed Father before, but never openly opposed him like this. It pained him.

Ulv gritted his teeth. He had made his decision. That was what made him sad. There was no way of knowing if or when he would see Father again. There was no anger in the old man’s face, just sorrow. That was even worse. Father used to get angry when Ulv disobeyed him, particularly if he put himself or others in danger. He seemed older than ever.

Father got up and walked towards Ulv. ‘I see you have made up your mind. Are you going to Sigurd Jarl?’

Ulv nodded, feeling a surge of disappointment. He got what he wanted, but he wished Father had offered more resistance. He could not find the words, so he was relieved when Father embraced him. They held each other while Ulv fought to hold back the tears.

With his head bowed, he pulled away, turned and went out the door. Outside, he swung the sack over his shoulder and grabbed his bow. After a dozen or so paces, he turned to look at Father in the doorway.

‘Are you going to Sigurd Jarl?’ Father repeated.

‘Yes, Father.’

Father nodded.

‘Goodbye, Father.’

‘Goodbye, my boy.’

Ulv found a spoon, wiped it on his tunic and tasted the

porridge. His memories of saying goodbye to Father had been too painful to dwell on. Did the old man want him to stay, or did he secretly prefer he left? It did not make sense. Father had prepared Ulv to fend for himself. They even went through years of combat training – quite unnecessary for a hunter living in the woods, according to Father.

Father advised him not to go raiding, but he also kept repeating that Ulv tended to do the opposite of what he recommended. Last winter, Father told dozens of stories about the world of warriors. It was almost as if he wanted Ulv to leave. But why? They lived a comfortable life and lacked nothing. Ulv contributed with more than his share of food and work. It simply did not make sense.

Ulv shook his head and stood up. Nothing had changed, and nothing good came out of feeling sorry for oneself. Ulv still had to fight for his place in this world, and now he knew how.

There was a battle to plan and prepare for.

CHAPTER 32: WALK

Neither birdsong nor the warmth of the April sun improved Marcus's mood. Bjarn was also sullen. They rode calmly along the north bank of the Blackwater. On several occasions, they met groups of monks transporting relics and valuables from the nearby churches and minor monasteries to the abbey of Kells, where the great battle was to take place. King Sechnall was in charge of the Irish forces, and Marcus would organise the monastery's defence until the reinforcements arrived.

Throughout the late winter and spring, they had been preparing for war. The monks repaired and strengthened the monastery walls and built platforms for archers. On the walls, they stored piles of rocks the size of a man's head, that the defenders could drop on enemies on the outside. They had cut and sharpened stakes, long as a man and thick as an arm, and dug them into the ground in front of vulnerable parts of the walls.

Blacksmiths forged hundreds of sharp iron caltrops. When strewn on the ground, they would rest on three finger-long spikes while a fourth pointed straight up and would do significant damage to animals or people who stepped on them. Marcus had also asked the blacksmith to produce the long and narrow arrowheads that Ulv had pilfered on the Orkneys. Their shape would allow them to penetrate deeper through a thick weapon shirt than the wider arrowheads the Irish used to hunt animals. Had Bjarn been pierced by a thin arrowhead the year before, he would not have survived the injury.

When the day came, men and women from the surrounding farms would gather to defend the monastery. But would that be enough?

Marcus made the sign of the cross over his chest, a gesture he had made a dozen times a day for the past six months. Attending masses and living so closely with the monks made him talk and act more like them. Maybe he was thinking and feeling more like them as well?

Marcus glanced at Bjarn and knew what he was thinking. There was a sadness inside them and in the air around them. Both knew with certainty that it would get even worse when one of them opened his mouth to speak.

Like Marcus and the others who had not taken the monastic vows, Bjarn wore the grey robes of a novice. His black hair was cut short, and his beard was shaved off. The wound was healed, and he endured the tedious masses without any seizures. He mumbled his prayers and performed his tasks to satisfaction. A few months earlier, Marcus had wondered if Bjarn was about to reject his pagan beliefs. But after their encounter with Ulv, the Northman had been quiet and kept more to himself.

Marcus understood, and dreaded this day. When Bjarn reined in his borrowed horse, he knew what was coming.

'Marcus …,' Bjarn began as their horses stood shoulder to shoulder.

Marcus looked at him without saying anything.

'I thank you for everything you have done for me, Marcus. I owe you my life.'

Marcus remained silent. Some conversations flowed better if the person who has something on their mind is allowed to finish talking.

'I tried to live in peace with the monks and learn about the White Christ. Maybe I could have gained his favour, with time.' Bjarn turned his gaze to the shore, towards Linn Duachaill.

'But you are preparing for war against my brothers. I have to choose sides ...'

Bjarn fell silent, as if he did not know how to complete the sentence.

'And you must choose them,' Marcus concluded for him.

Bjarn nodded.

'You have made your choice, Bjarn. I cannot say that I hope we meet again soon, because then we will be at war. But I do wish you a safe journey, by the grace of the Lord.'

'The Lord's grace be with you, too,' replied the Northman. It sounded unnatural, and his face twisted as if he had eaten seaweed.

'Nice try!' Marcus smiled. It felt better now that the pus was out of the wound. 'Now, walk away.'

Bjarn laughed and turned the horse.

'*Walk*, I said!' Marcus's voice was stern.

Bjarn looked back at him with a surprised expression.

'I cannot blame you for choosing your brothers over me. But you cannot steal the abbot's horse before my eyes,' Marcus continued.

Bjarn blushed.

'I advise you to walk as slowly as possible, to regrow your beard before your warmongering friends notice your red baby cheeks.'

Bjarn laughed again. Then, he slid down from the horse, gave the reins to Marcus and left.

Marcus sat quietly on his horse and watched his friend disappear among the bushes by the river. Out of sight and out of his life. Like his father and mother, Julia and Ulv. He was alone again.

Marcus dismounted and unfastened the two bundles of blankets attached on either side of his horse. From one, he pulled out a shovel. He found a suitable spot on the north side of a dead tree and dug a pit, one foot wide and almost as long as himself. When the hole was knee-deep, a meshwork of roots made the digging difficult. Marcus chopped at the roots with the spade, but the shovel was not a helpful tool for such work. The dull edges required him to chop at the same spot several times.

'Do you need help with your grave?' sounded a voice.

For a moment, Marcus thought that it was Bjarn who had returned, but that was not possible. The man spoke Celtic.

Marcus jumped out of his pit and turned towards the sound. A dark-haired man with a bow over his shoulder and a long knife in his belt. His garments were worn, stained with mud. Or blood? The stranger's gaze fell on the rolled-up blanket between them.

Marcus regretted his reaction. Surely, it revealed that what lay in the tattered blanket was of value to him. When he looked up, he met a stern, scrutinising gaze.

'Where are you from, monk?' the stranger asked. His right hand calmly stroked the outside of the thigh, inches from the bone hilt of his knife.

'Kells!' replied Marcus, a little too eagerly. He tried again, calmer this time. 'I'm a novice at Kells.'

Intense eyes drilled into Marcus, attempting to see through him in search of the truth. The hand lay on the hilt of the bone knife.

'I see a foreigner who claims he is from Kells, dressed in grey monk's robes. He is alone but rides two horses. In the blanket between us lies a long and narrow item that he intends to conceal. Who is this man who pretends to be a monk? Who owns the sword he wants to bury? And, who rode the other horse?'

Marcus examined the stranger as he thought. There was something wild about the young man, his clothes, his face, his eyes. The man seemed torn to pieces by grief and anger.

'It's a long story, my friend,' Marcus replied, handing him the spade.

CHAPTER 33: COAL

Julia coughed up brown mucus while waiting for her turn to be lowered in the shaft. Mildred and Durwin had descended before her, as always. She shoved the tiny piece of bread in her mouth without dividing it. The miners received their breakfast at sunrise. If they arrived late, they got nothing. There was hot soup for dinner, and at sunset, they got bread and vegetables before going home.

Spring was the worst time of the year for those who starved. The grain stores were depleted, and the pieces of bread were getting smaller every day. Besides, they were full of sand. Any fruit was consumed months ago, and the vegetables were half-rotten. Dried onions lasted the longest, making them the staple of the miners' diet.

A stone's throw away, birds greeted the morning sun with their song. The forest was full of life after the winter gloom, but the animals were safe from Julia. Even an experienced hunter could search for several days without felling a deer, and Julia had never learned to use a bow. Cwen had begun teaching her how to set traps, but Julia returned to Wucestre before she had time to master the skill. Also, as she worked from sunrise to sunset every day, except Sundays, there was not much time to set traps.

She nodded to the sun before being lowered into the shaft. It would be dark again before she got back up.

The shaft was four man-lengths deep. Many years ago, there was coal at the surface in this area, and people extracted it for their own use. But Lord Edric hired men to dig for larger deposits. When they unearthed a rich layer of coal, they expanded the shaft to the sides. In these low tunnels, the children worked. The youngest had seen six or seven winters, like Durwin. His job was to crawl back and forth through the tunnels with leather straps over his shoulders, pulling coal wagons without wheels.

Open flames were dangerous in the mines, so they had nothing but a few wax candles to help them find their way through the tunnels. If a light went out, a child could be alone in a tight hole in pitch darkness, with rats as the only company. The miners, who were all children, were not allowed to talk to each other in the mines. The Mongrel took care of that. He was the only adult worker in the mines, and the only one who did not do any work. His duty was to kick and yell at any child who crossed his path.

Julia was one of the largest workers in the newest of the two mines. Therefore, she was assigned the task of loading coal from the wagons into the barrels that were hoisted up the shaft. The horses on the surface walked in circles all day, pulling the ropes that lifted the barrels. Twice, Julia barely evaded fully loaded barrels that came loose or broke in the shaft above her, so she learned to take a few steps back while waiting for the barrel to be emptied and lowered again.

Throughout the winter, she had shovelled coal from morning to nightfall. The shortage of food made her thin and sinewy, and she no longer had the curves of a woman. It did not bother her, for she had seen what kind of attention other girls received. A pretty face could make life easier in many places. The mines were not among them.

As far as Julia knew, the Mongrel had not yet put his filthy paws on Mildred, but it was only a question of time. At first, Julia thought a girl in her tenth winter was too young to be a victim of the unwelcome attention of such predators, but she soon learned that the hideous overseer's depraved desires were not limited by age. Therefore, Julia always paid attention to which tunnel Mildred worked, and kept close to her when she came to the shaft to drink.

Between the sessions of shovelling coal, Julia pondered how she would defend herself if the Mongrel came after her or Mildred. The children working in the mines were not allowed to carry knives, so she had no weapons. A pointed stone could serve the same purpose, so Julia had collected suitable stones and placed them at strategic locations around. The best was shaped like a large spearhead and lay next to the water barrel a few paces away from her. She could barely make it out in the fading light from the shaft above, as another day of work drew to a close.

Although months of hard labour made her stronger, her back and joints ached more than before. With a grimace, she grabbed the shovel and unloaded the last wooden wagon. When the barrel was full, she jerked at the ropes to signal that it was ready to be hoisted up. Moments later, one of the boys shouted 'Ya!' to make the horse walk. When the barrel was on its way up the shaft, the Mongrel struck his knife against his tin mug, indicating the workday was over.

Julia walked around to the tunnels and shouted into each of them to make sure every child got out. Those who worked furthest away might not hear the signal over the noise of tapping chisels. At first, she had made sure that Mildred and Durwin returned safely, but after she had learned the names of every child who worked in the mine, she ensured that everybody else got up before her. This day, as was often the case, she had to climb the ropes unassisted because the boys who drove the horses had gone home. The sun had set before Julia pulled herself out of the shaft. A thin, red stripe on the horizon was all that remained of the daylight. Tomorrow was Sunday, and everybody had time off. Julia planned to put out some snares in the woods after church. But first, she needed to eat and sleep. She walked to the shed where the Mongrel handed out payments for the day's work and smiled when she saw that there was a whole piece of bread on the table next to him.

'Here!' the Mongrel said and pressed a cracked onion in

her hand.

'Thank you,' Julia replied, hesitantly.

'Thank you, too. Now, begone!' replied the butcher.

'May I have my bread first?'

'You're too late. There is no more bread.'

'No, there is one right there,' Julia replied and pointed to the round bread on the table.

'It's mine. You have received your payment,' the Mongrel replied with a horrible smile.

'You gave me a rotten onion!' Julia yelled.

'You don't deserve more than a rotten onion!'

'Give me my bread!' Julia demanded, fuming.

'It's my bread. Leave, before I hurt you!'

'You steal our food!' Julia looked around for somebody who could support her against this injustice, but she was alone.

'And there's nothing you can do about it, you filthy rat!' He tilted his head and measured her from head to toe. 'I look forward to seeing you again on Monday,' he added with a smile.

Julia trembled with anger and fear, and tears welled up in her eyes. She was alone with this brutal man on the outskirts of the village after sunset, and suddenly felt insecure.

'I'm going to tell the priest about you tomorrow!' she said and ran home to Esme.

CHAPTER 34: HORSES

Marcus climbed up the east wall as soon as the Mass of *prime* was over. He put his hand to his forehead to shield his eyes from the sun. Between Kells and the coast were several columns of smoke. The Vikings of Linn Duachaill were on the move. The day had come!

He turned to the monastery courtyard and shouted.

'Light the beacon and ring the bells!'

His heart pounded as he ran towards the nearest tower. Today was the day when they would defeat the heathens or die trying.

'Cearan!' Marcus stopped when he saw the abbot in the square below.

'Abbot Cearan,' Marcus corrected himself when he remembered who he was addressing, 'may I offer a proposal for your consideration?'

'Lay brother Marcus,' the abbot replied politely, 'what would you ask of me?'

'The beacons are lit. The heathens are on their way. May I suggest you take with you anyone unfit or unwilling to fight and ride to the priory of Bellach-Duin?'

'Yes,' replied the abbot, 'we'll take with us our most important scriptures and relics and ride west after vespers.' The abbot made the sign of the cross. 'I leave the defence of the monastery to you, Marcus of Northumbria. May the Lord grant you wisdom and fortitude.'

'Thank you,' Marcus replied, unsure of how to respond to

such blessings. A marvellous joy swelled inside him as he ran on the wall and shouted instructions to monks and lay brothers. Under his leadership, they would repel the Vikings.

'Marcus Maximus,' he whispered while the church bells rang to call the farmers in the area to defence. He immediately realised he was committing a great sin. If they won the battle, it was because God wanted it so, not because Marcus was a great army commander. He fell on his knees and prayed for the Lord's forgiveness for his blasphemous arrogance.

When he arose, he was calmer. As he continued his inspection of the wall, he took the time to talk to those he met, encourage them and make sure they were familiar with their assignments in the forthcoming battle.

Marcus climbed the south-eastern tower and looked out over the area. The forests had been cleared decades ago, so the monastery was surrounded by green meadows. There was little or nothing for an enemy to hide behind. The flaw was that the walls were no taller than two man-lengths in several places, and the Northmen would have little difficulty scaling them.

Marcus had overseen the improvement of the defensive measures around those weak spots. Enemies charging the monastery risked severe injuries to their feet if they trod on any of the hundreds of sharp caltrops hidden in the grass, or they might impale themselves on the pointed wooden stakes protruding at an acute angle in front of the walls. Beyond these obstacles, a score of monks and archers hid behind the walls, with barrels with spears and arrows.

The gates were reinforced with thick logs on the inside. Barrels of caltrops and oil stood ready to be overturned if the enemy attacked there. A painful death awaited the first to try to enter through the gates.

What was still missing was men. Or women, for that matter. The perimeter of the wall was too long for them to man each section. The Irish were stretched too thin, and without more defenders on the walls, the enemy could break through anywhere. They might lose a handful of warriors, but as soon as the enemy was within the walls, their strength and fighting prowess would be decisive.

Time passed quickly. Marcus spent the morning inspecting the fortifications. When the farmers from the surrounding farmsteads arrived, he ensured that everybody got an axe, a spear or a bow, and instructed them on where and how they would contribute to the defence.

During the sexts Mass at midday, Marcus stood alone on the wall and watched the rider approaching. He went down to greet him at the gate.

'They come! The Northmen are coming!' shouted the young Irishman from horseback. It was evident from the mare's gait and laboured breath that it had been pushed to its limits.

Marcus took the reins of the horse and handed a waterskin to the young rider.

'We know that. We have seen the smoke from the beacons, and we have rung the bells. Before vespers, we will have several hundred archers on the walls, and the heathens will charge to their death. Provided they even survive the voyage up the river.'

The rider drank eagerly but spat out the water when he heard what Marcus was saying.

'You do not understand! It is not the beacons that are burning; it is the farms! The Northmen don't row their ships up the river. They have horses! They arrive before the Mass at nons!'

CHAPTER 35: PRELUDE

There was not much time to prepare. The next day smoke rose in the east. Not long after, the monastery church bells tolled, and the activity picked up in the woods. Ulv took Jarl with him and climbed a nearby hill. From there, they had a good overview of the area towards the river in the north. It was not long before they saw men moving through the forest. A group of four passed nearby. An elderly man, a middle-aged man and two younger men. Maybe a family with three generations. They wore simple woollen clothes and carried primitive weapons. The grandfather had a large scythe, while the father and one of the sons each carried an axe. The fourth bore a hunting bow and a knife. They were farmers who gathered to defend the monastery.

Ulv and Jarl returned to the camp, where Ulv packed what they needed and hid the rest inside the cave. He hoped nobody would stumble across the place while they were away. Not sure if he would get the chance to come back, he also put the few things he had of value in the belt pouch. Giving Jarl plenty of food, he made sure the large dog did not get distracted by an empty stomach. He draped the cloak over his shoulders and picked up the axe and his other weapons. Patting Jarl, he looked around at what had been his home most of the winter. After a few moments, he turned his back on the camp, satisfied that he had what he needed for the coming battle.

They set course for the ford in the north and rushed

off. On their way through the forest, they came across several groups of men going in the same direction. However, they had no problem avoiding detection. Ulv knew the area well after countless hunting trips over the past year. Of course, Jarl's keen senses also helped. Apart from Geir Galne, nobody had surprised Ulv for a long time. That experience, on the other hand, had been a wake-up call. Now he knew that he could not blindly trust Jarl in such cases. He had to keep his own senses sharpened as well.

Arriving at the ford at the River Blackwater, Ulv discovered a problem. He was not the only one who intended to cross the river. From a copse of trees, he could see small groups of people coming from different directions with course for the same part of the river. Impatient, Ulv did not want to wait for a potential opening with fewer people. It was impossible to know whether the stem of people would decrease or whether there would only be more Irishmen. Would people understand that he was not on their side if they saw him? Jarl would help in that matter. If nothing else, the dog belonged there. Ulv came to think of Vass's argument when they went in behind the palisades in Dyflin to find the leader and stop the senseless slaughter. When Ulv had indicated that Vass did not look particularly Irish, the stoic warrior had pointed out that even if somebody suspected that a Northman was among them, nobody would confront them for fear that they might be right. Ulv decided to follow Vass's way of thinking. He strung the bow, pulled the hood over his head and set off with deliberate steps towards the ford. Although he would have preferred to have both hands free when crossing the river, he chose to keep the bow in his left hand. The plan was to get over between two groups that were approaching.

The plan worked. Ulv and Jarl were on their way out into the river when the first group had just come over. Shortly after, a shout sounded behind them. The language was incomprehensible, and Ulv pretended not to notice. Instead, he concentrated on getting Jarl to jump off a rock and into the deep water. The shout came again. Ulv turned. Three men approached, and their eyes were on him. There was no doubt about who they had called at. The men were young. One giant of a man carrying a pitchfork, another had a bow over his shoulder. The third man, carrying a sword at the hip, said something. Ulv gestured. First, he held a finger in front of his mouth, then he pointed down the river.

At last, he held out an arm towards the bank on the other side. The men looked down at the river and then at each other. As Ulv turned to continue across, it dawned on him that he had misjudged the situation. Vass seemed like somebody you did not want to mess with. If you had a friend or two with you, the young wolfskin was still one you would rather avoid confronting. If, on the other hand, you were nervous about the ensuing battle, and you saw an easy prey. An easy target that was all alone, while you had two mates with you – one of which bigger and stronger than the neighbour's bull ...

Ulv looked at the men who had come ashore on the other side. None of them appeared to have bows. Thank Odin for the small gifts in life. The man with the sword shouted again, and the men on the other side turned. Ulv kept wading and spoke calmly to Jarl, who had started growling. Several of the men were shouting, and Ulv realised that this would not end without blood. He drew an arrow, nocked it and spun around towards the men behind him. An instant later, the Irishman with the bow cried out. The arrow protruded from his left forearm. Ulv turned, drew another shaft and let it fly. The man on the right screamed and reached for his foot, where the arrow sat just above the knee. When the men moved their gaze from their injured comrade and back to Ulv, he was ready with another shaft on the string. He spoke calmly to Jarl, before shouting:

'I'll put the next arrow in your throat. Turn around, go home and thank the gods you pray to for saving your life today. In the other direction, only death awaits.'

The men on the river bank probably understood as little

of what he said as he had understood from their cries, but it was not of much consequence. The two arrows that had put two of them out of play, and the third that was ready on the bow, spoke a language everybody understood.

If nobody did anything stupid, everybody would be able to walk or be carried away alive. Ulv kept talking to Jarl as they continued across the river and came up on the other side. The arrow aimed at the men in front of him, but all signs of resistance seemed to have left them. One man had taken off his shirt and tore a piece of it. The other looked alternately at the injured man and at Ulv as if he did not dare to move. These were men who would become his enemies later in the day, but Ulv did not want to kill them. Not here, not now. He hoped they would turn around, all six, and that he would never see them again.

He hoped he had done everybody a favour. That they would survive and that less blood would be spilt in the coming battle.

Ulv and Jarl stalked off towards the monastery. Ulv was not known in this area. It was more densely populated and not suitable for hunting. He expected to arrive at the abbey before the Northmen. If so, he would scout the area. Still outlawed, he would need the support of Geir Galne to not be as vulnerable among his own as he was among the Irish. And even if he got to Galne before some of the others decided to take his life, it would be an advantage if he had something else he could contribute with. Such as information about what the surrounding area looked like. With that in mind, he set off due north to circle the monastery from the east at a reasonable distance.

Not long after, he came across tracks from horses – many horses, heading straight for the monastery.

Of course. The Northmen had understood that the river would be watched, so they had taken the road overland. With horses, they would avoid the ambush and arrive sooner than expected. There was no point circling around the monastery. He had to find the Northmen. Find Geir Galne, without anyone seeing him first. Neither Irishmen nor Northmen.

Ulv followed the horse tracks through the forest until he could see the monastery through the trees in front of him. A stone's throw further, the forest had been cleared, and out in the meadow between the trees and the monastery, a small army of horsemen had gathered. There had to be over a hundred men. Of course, there were guards around the place, and it did not take long before Ulv saw the first one. He took Jarl with him and crawled under the shade of a large tree with low branches. Moments later, he saw the guard moving north for a while, where he raised his hand to somebody before returning. Then he did the same thing to the south.

Ulv had to make a couple of decisions. First, he had to decide whether to report for duty or to try to sneak past. If he contacted the guard, he could only hope that Geir Galne would intervene before he was taken to Kjetil Korte. If he stalked past, he was even more vulnerable if he was discovered. Nobody with good intentions snuck into a camp. And what was he to do with Jarl?

Keeping to the shadows, he kept watching the area, but when the guard returned from his second round, Ulv crept forward towards the meadow. Jarl lay down. Ulv had given the command to stay. An exercise Jarl had done many times before, but never for any length of time. It was not an option to tether him. He would be helpless if anyone found him and wanted to hurt him. Ulv did not know the consequences, but it was the best he came up with.

He moved from bushes, tufts and trees on the edge of the forest. Heading towards where the guard had stopped and turned, he stalked forward. Suddenly the heather to his right rattled. Ulv forced himself to stay calm. He sat down and looked in the direction of the sound. A man came walking towards him, probably one of the sentries. Maybe thirty steps away. Ulv stayed still, his eyes locked on the sentry. Twenty steps now. Ten. The man glanced around. He slowed down. Stopped.

And turned.

Ulv let out his breath, waited until the man was a few steps away, then he crept on. He could not wait much longer, as the other sentry would soon come. Moments later, Ulv could breathe easier within the circle of guards.

Once there, Ulv pulled the hood over his head to cover his blonde hair and walked with as much confidence he could muster out of the woods towards the riders on the plain. His eyes searched for familiar figures as he tried to keep his head cool and his movements natural. Two men carrying shields came walking straight towards him, and Ulv noticed them too late to change course. They nodded to Ulv as they passed, and he nodded back. The sounds of footsteps faded, and Ulv closed his eyes for a moment and grimaced. *Do not say anything. Just, let me go. Do not say anything!*

'Hey, you!' sounded a voice behind him.

Ulv slowed down and stopped. He looked at the ground and sighed before he turned around. The man had moved his hand to the axe in his belt and stared at Ulv. 'Where do you think you're going?'

'I have important information for Geir Galne,' Ulv replied.

'Galne is not in charge here. Kjetil Jarl is the one you bring information to. But you might not be so interested in talking to him?' The man's eyes narrowed.

'I can talk to the Jarl. No problem. Just show me the way to Galne first.'

The man glanced at his companion and pulled his axe. The other man changed his grip on the spear he carried and aimed it at Ulv.

'You will come with us, whelp.' He spit the last word like a rotten piece of fruit.

Ulv held out his hands. It would be useless to resist. No matter how a fight went, it was going to end in a loss. Squirming only made things worse when you are stuck in the net.

With a spearpoint to his back, Ulv crossed the last stretch towards the men gathered west of the monastery. *Where was Galne?* Ulv's stomach twisted when he glimpsed a prominent figure with blonde hair towering over the other Northmen. *Kjetil Korte. The Jarl. Or was it Flatnose now? Flatnose Jarl?* Ulv considered insulting the Jarl, but it would be foolish if he carried any hope of surviving the day. Survival was hardly a likely outcome, anyway. Ulv was an intruder brought to face the man who declared him an outlaw. Kjetil was now a Jarl and did not answer to anyone.

By Odin's ravens, life had seen brighter moments.

'Hey, cuckoo, where are you taking him?'

Ulv had never before been so happy to hear the hoarse voice of Geir Galne. His captors turned to face Galne, who came walking towards them.

'I'm taking him to the *Jarl*,' said the spearman, with emphasis on *Jarl*.

'Put away your weapons before I make porridge out of your guts.' Galne's voice was louder now. 'Did he not instruct you to bring him to me?' Galne glanced at Ulv.

Ulv nodded. The two men looked at each other and lowered their weapons.

'So why didn't you do that?' Galne continued towards the two men who were still holding weapons. The berserk did not stop until he stood with his face a handbreadth from the man with the axe.

'Geeet lost!' he hissed in his face.

The warriors backed away and left.

'Ulv!' Geir Galne said with a smile. 'Good to see you.'

He sounded strangely sincere. Ulv did not know how to respond. Not that it mattered, as Galne had words enough for both of them. 'Listen, Flatnose Jarl will soon come trampling as only he can trample. Let me do the talking.'

Ulv was going to answer, but he was not quick enough. Galne continued:

'Understood? Be a good boy and keep quiet, and I'll get you through this day alive!'

Ulv nodded, but then recalled that he had important information to share. 'But ...'

'Hush, doggy! Hush!' Galne interrupted. 'Come on.' He patted his thigh as he set off towards the men and Kjetil Korte.

Quite right. Kjetil Korte came trampling. Ulv realised that he had put his life in the hands of the most erratic man he knew.

'What is this supposed to mean?' asked the imposing Jarl.

'Kjetil Jarl,' replied Galne, bowing his head. 'Yes, this is Ulv, and yes, I know he's an outlaw. But this is not Dyflin. This is the area he has been banished to. And, yes, we can kill him, but we might as well wait until we don't need him anymore.'

Ulv glanced at Galne, clinging to the hope this was one of his clearer moments.

'Need him?' asked the Jarl.

'Yes, Ulv has told me he can open the monastery gates for us.'

Ulv's mouth dropped as he stared at the berserk. Galne continued:

'Besides, he comes with vital information. We should launch the attack as soon as possible. Reinforcements are swarming in from the surrounding countryside, and the longer we wait, the more Irishmen we'll have to fight.'

Ulv recovered control over his body, but he was still surprised. *How did Galne know what information Ulv carried? Did he figure it out on his own, or did he just want to get the battle going?*

'We create a distraction with a frontal assault, and Ulv sneaks in and opens the gates for us. Come the second wave, we charge through the open gates. We can take it from there, wouldn't you say?' continued the berserk.

Kjetil Jarl stared at Galne. With a brief glance at Ulv, he shook his head and sighed. 'Come, Galne, we have an attack to plan.'

CHAPTER 36: 126

Marcus glanced over his shoulder to the west. From his position on the east wall, he could not see Abbot Cearan and his entourage, but they would still be visible from some of the higher towers. With eyes closed, he asked the Lord to hold his hand over them.

When he opened them again, he looked to the east, towards the heathens who came riding across the meadows, closing in on the monastery in a loose formation.

'Close the gates!' he commanded. 'Reinforce them with timber and brace them with more logs. Empty a barrel of caltrops outside. Wait with the oil.'

'But, Brother,' objected Brother Máedóc, 'more men are coming from the farms. We cannot shut them out!'

Marcus had seen several men coming from the north and the west. But he could not risk the Northmen riding straight in through the gate to the south. 'We have to make do with those we have. Close the gate!'

Máedóc nodded and conveyed the command.

Two dozen monks and lay brothers remained in the monastery. During the day, they had been reinforced by thirty-nine men, eight women and some children. All were divided into groups of eight or nine, armed and deployed on the wall. One group on the west wall and one in the north. Four groups on the east wall and one group on each side of the south gate. Everybody sat on the newly built platforms, hidden behind the parapet. Marcus did not want them to reveal their positions. In addition, he had placed the two best archers in the tower in the monastery courtyard.

It would not be enough. The heathens, who were no more than a couple of bowshots away from the east wall, had twice their number. Marcus scouted to the south, towards the forest and the River Blackwater, but found no comfort. All his plans were based on the Northmen rowing up the river. The Irish were supposed to attack the ships all day, weakening them before reaching the monastery. Sechnall would come from the south with a hundred men before evening.

Alas, the Northmen had ridden overland instead and arrived long before noon. And a half-day earlier than Sechnall was expected. If the monastery fell, the heathens would hold the wall against the Irish in the evening. The damned horses ruined the whole plan. How could the Northmen suddenly have horses?

The enemy stopped out of reach of the Irish bows.

'One hundred and twenty-six men,' said the monk next to him. It was probably accurate, as Donnchadh was good with numbers. They were too many. But a commander could not show fear with the enemy at the gates. Marcus patted Donnchadh on the shoulder. 'Thank you, my friend. Then we know what it takes to win.'

Crouched and concealed from the riders in the fields, he ran from group to group on the east wall and at the gate. To each of them, he said the same thing:

'The heathens are only two for each of us. We hold the wall, and that gives us an advantage. Some of them will be injured by the traps before they reach the wall. If each of us kills one man with the first arrow, we are ahead before the battle begins. Do not reveal yourself until they are close enough that you can hear their breath. Hold your shots until you are sure to hit. Our task is to stop the first attack. When they retreat, Sechnall will hit them from behind and annihilate them.'

The frightened defenders nodded and smiled bravely below fearful eyes.

Marcus shook off the gnawing feeling of shame on his way back to his position by the tower where the east wall met the south. It did not sound so complicated when presented in that way, but the new plan had some prerequisites one could not rely on. First of all, it was unlikely that each of the Irishmen could kill an attacker before he reached the wall. The Irish bows were made to hunt animals, not penetrate armour or many layers of thick cloth. In addition, the Northmen wore large shields that protected their head, neck and upper body when they advanced. They also had their own bows and spears and were far more accurate than most of the Irish who hid behind the parapet.

The chance that they would repel the first attack was so slim that Marcus did not worry that Sechnall was not around.

'Men of Kells!'

Somebody shouted from the outside, and Marcus got up to look over the edge of the east wall. A man stood alone on the plain between the Northmen and the wall. He spoke Celtic, probably a slave, or one of the many Irishmen who collaborated with the blonde strangers.

'Kjetil Jarl sets his terms as follows,' the Irishman continued. 'Surrender the escaped slave Marcus of Northumbria. He is a niding and will be judged by the Jarl. Everybody else is granted free passage out of the monastery and can come back before sunset.'

It went completely quiet on both sides of the wall. Marcus did not dare look at any of the Irish around him. He made an effort to recognise the Northmen in the meadow. The big man with blonde hair under his helmet had to be Kjetil. The Jarl. The warriors around him were probably his hird. He did not know their names, but neither were men he wanted to get to know better. He was looking for Magnus Trygg. Did he live? What about Bjarn? Was he the one who had told Kjetil that Marcus was here? Was Ulv among them, or was he still banished to the wilderness?

'Perhaps we should accept the offer from the Jarl?' sounded a voice to Marcus's right. Máedóc's voice. The monk continued: 'Our young commander here had no objections to closing the gates to brave men and women who came to fight with us. His only intention is to save himself. Is it God's will that we all die for a foreign slave? This is their battle, not ours. Yet, his plans brought the heathens to our gates. The Lord punishes us for giving him a room in his house.'

'Maybe you could ask for thirty silver with that deal, Máedóc?' Donnchadh replied.

'You cannot believe the haughty boy to be the son of God?' Máedóc spat.

'No, but I'm starting to wonder if you are our Judas, brother Máedóc!' Donnchadh shot back.

This did not bode well. Even before a single man had fallen, before one arrow had been released, the will to fight was at the breaking point. Marcus had to take charge once more. He straightened his back and shouted in Celtic:

'I'm Marcus, son of Gaius, a merchant from Northumbria. If my life could buy freedom for my brothers and sisters, I would gladly give it up in the name of the Lord. But it would be a great sin to hand over this abbey to the heathens just to save our own lives. Our souls will be condemned to eternal torment for our betrayal.'

After a short silence, Máedóc fell to his knees and bowed his head. 'Marcus, son of Gaius, is a man in the Lord's grace, sharing in His infinite wisdom. I realise my mistake and my sin. Fear led me astray. Forgive me, brothers.'

'The Lord alone can forgive you, brother Máedóc. Today we fight in His name and die with pure hearts if that is His will,' Marcus concluded.

The monks around them closed their eyes and made the sign of the cross. Some of the farmers who had arrived during the day did the same. So was the first puny attack repelled – the assault on the defenders' unity and courage.

The Irishman who spoke for the Northmen went back to the Jarl. Marcus could hear laughter, but not what was said. Kjetil Jarl began to ride along the line of men and give orders. Soon, three groups of eight to ten riders broke out from the crowd and sped off in different directions to the north and northwest. Two other groups began riding around the monastery, in opposite directions and outside of shooting range.

CHAPTER 37: PLAN

Ulv stayed in the background when Kjetil Jarl gathered his men a few bowshots from the monastery. A wall encircled the monastery, but it was not very high. Two men could easily scale it together. From a tower where the east wall met the south wall, a skilled archer could do a lot of damage. Ulv hoped the Irish did not have too many of those.

After a while, an Irishman in Kjetil Jarl's company approached the walls, and there was a shouted exchange of incomprehensible words. The debate was still ongoing, when Geir Galne returned.

'What's happening?' asked Ulv.

'Flatnose Jarl sent an Irishman to negotiate,' said Galne.

'About what?' asked Ulv.

'I expect our benevolent Jarl will offer the Irish a chance to survive if they hand over your thrall.'

'Marcus is dead if they take that deal.'

'Yes, but it's not that simple. It's never that simple.'

'What happens next, then?'

'The monks will refuse, eventually. Flatnose will then dispatch bands of riders to capture some Irish hostages and threaten to kill them unless the monks surrender. That won't work either, but it will give the servants of the White Christ some much-needed fighting spirit. Eventually, we will attack. I have recommended diversionary attacks from several sides. That will reveal if they have enough men to defend all sides, and it will allow you to enter unseen. Only the gods know how it ends.'

'Do they really expect me to open the gate from the inside?'

'It doesn't matter what they expect. It is your chance to prove your worth as a warrior and make up for past failures. What you are able to do once inside is another matter. You will also have an opportunity to get your thrall out of there before Flatnose caves his skull in.'

'Well, then,' Ulv sighed, 'I'd better get ready. I'll find a good spot and wait for the right moment.'

Galne nodded and left.

Ulv was deep in thought when Bjarn slapped a hand on his shoulder.

'Ulv,' the short-haired Northman greeted him.

'Bjarn! Are you here?'

The Northman appeared like a warrior once more. He wore a weapon shirt under his tunic, and a shield hung on his back. Under his right arm, he held a bundle.

'Of course. Did you think I had become witless and willing to spend my life kneeling on stone floors?' Bjarn smiled, but it soon faded as if it dawned on him that he might not want an answer to that question.

'Look, I have something for you.' Bjarn handed Ulv the bundle. 'I heard somebody say you were going into the monastery.'

Ulv unfolded the bundle and recognised the monk's robes.

'Wearing these, you won't stand out like a lamb in the chicken pen,' Bjarn said. 'Maybe you can reach Marcus and get him out of there before we attack? He saved my life, Ulv.' Bjarn's expression was sombre.

'I'll see what I can do, Bjarn.'

Another familiar figure approached them – a fair-haired

wolfskin.

'Ulv!' Vass said with a grin.

'Vass! Good to see you!'

The wolfskin embraced him. When they were at arm's length again, he was still grinning. 'I hear you're going inside the walls again. I'm afraid I can't go with you this time.'

'It wasn't my idea this time, either,' replied Ulv.

'No? I didn't believe what I heard when they said you were here. Not until they told me about the plan. Then I was sure it was you!'

'It was Geir Galne's plan, and he offered my services to Kjetil Jarl.' Ulv shook his head.

'Ha ha! If it wasn't your plan, it had to be his! But keep calm. I'll jump that wall and help you as soon as we get started.'

'Looking forward to seeing you there. Now, I have to get ready.'

'See you inside,' said Vass.

Ulv set off towards the monastery. He had to find a place to enter. Somewhere the Irish did not watch that closely. Once inside, he would just open the gates, find Marcus, persuade him to come with him and get them both out alive.

Easy.

Ulv shook his head and put on the grey robes.

CHAPTER 38: DEAL

A long, quiet period followed. Marcus took the opportunity to walk along the wall. He pretended to inspect the fortifications and showed with a smile or a nod that he was satisfied. Each time he came to a new group of defenders, he stopped and talked to them. He praised their courage and assured them that the Lord would grant them victory. A girl who had not seen more than eight or nine winters clung to her mother. Tears ran down her cheeks, but she did not let out a single whimper.

Marcus climbed down from the wall, found some fist-sized stones in the monastery yard and climbed back up to the girl.

'What is your name, young lady?' he asked.

'Betha,' the girl replied in a low voice.

'That is a beautiful name. It means "life", right?'

The girl nodded.

'Do you know why the Lord has given you that very name, Betha?'

The girl shook her head.

'It's because you're the most important of us. You are the one who gives us life. Because you are here, we shall all live.'

The girl smiled and nodded. A blush spread over her cheeks.

'Do you remember David? The little shepherd boy?' Marcus continued.

The girl nodded again. 'He killed the giant!'

'Just so!' replied Marcus. 'Do you remember what David used to kill him?'

'A stone!' the girl replied, beaming with pride.

'Yes, that's right. Stones are God's weapon against evil giants. Take these stones and give a few to your brother. If a giant pops his ugly head over the edge, throw a stone at him, just like David did. Can you do that?'

The girl grinned and nodded like a woodpecker.

'Thank you,' her mother said softly.

'Thank you,' Marcus replied and moved on.

*

When Marcus reached the east wall, the first group of enemy riders returned. The Northmen gathered around them, and a loud discussion ensued. The big man Marcus assumed to be Kjetil Jarl hauled something from the horse of one of the newcomers, hung it over his shoulder and walked over the meadow towards the monastery wall. Forty steps away from where Marcus stood, he threw the bundle to the ground. It began to squirm in the grass. Kjetil bent to remove a sack and pulled a young boy up by his hair. The child screamed and stretched his toes down towards the ground.

Kjetil drew his sword and pressed it against the boy's neck. The boy went silent.

'Marcus *Niding*!' Kjetil called, using the Norse word for coward, 'I haven't bothered learning the islanders' silly chirping sounds. You understand what I'm saying, so you can relay it to those doomed White Christ weaklings when they're done pissing themselves. At my signal, one of my men will ride around the little sheep fence you hide behind. When he's back with us, I'll cut off this boy's head. When he's dead, I'll fetch the next captive and send out a new rider. For each round, I'll throw another head over the wall. Only you can stop it. Their lives are in your hands.'

Kjetil Flatnose raised his hand, and a rider set off at a gallop.

'Shall we shoot?' whispered one of the archers crouched nearby.

'No,' Marcus replied. 'The Jarl is well protected by his chain mail, his padded shirt and his helmet, and he knows that very well. If we show weakness, they will only do more of this. Keep low until you are ordered to shoot. They do not know what defence we have, and that is why they hesitate. They are trying to get us to reveal our strengths and weaknesses.'

Then, he relayed the Jarl's words and repeated his command that everybody should keep low and still.

The Jarl had the advantage and tried to force a quick surrender or a desperate move from the Irish. If disembodied heads began to appear in the monastery yard, fear and despair would spread among the monks and farmers on the walls. Defeat would not be far off.

Marcus had to find a countermeasure.

He grabbed a nearby rope and fastened it around a pole on the platform. Without heeding the monks' objections, he lowered himself to the outside. Unarmed, he walked towards the large Jarl, who was still holding the whining boy by the hair.

'Greetings, Flatnose Jarl. It's good to see that power has not made you arrogant. You still pick opponents who are half your size!' Marcus tilted his head and looked at the red-haired boy. With a worried expression, he added, 'But they keep getting younger. And unarmed. The defeats against Ulv and me has made you more … careful?'

Kjetil released the boy, raised his sword and took three quick steps towards Marcus. Frightened cries sounded from the monastery.

Marcus forced himself to stand still. Even Kjetil was not stupid enough to kill the man he negotiated with. Nobody would trust him or his people again, and his time as Jarl would be over.

At least he *hoped* that Kjetil was not that stupid.

Kjetil stopped. Marcus thanked God.

'That's a pretty sword, Flatnose. Did you find it in a ditch?' Marcus asked with feigned admiration.

Kjetil's eyes narrowed. He did not seem to be as angry as he used to be. More inquisitive. It almost seemed as if he was *thinking*.

'Where is your own blade? I remember it. Well balanced, with precious gems on the hilt. All in all, a beautiful sword.'

'What are you trying to achieve, thrall? Before the sun sets, you're all dead. You, the boy here, and all your weakling friends.'

'Maybe so. But then, you will never see your sword again. I have hidden it, and I will exchange it for the lives of the boy and the other Irish you have taken from the farms. A man who kills women and children is a man without honour. Your men will talk about you behind your back, and the gods will mock you. Nobody will respect such a man, and nobody will follow such a Jarl. That is why I will repeat my offer. Release the Irish, and you will get your sword back. If you hurt but one of them, you will never see it again.'

Kjetil went silent. Jaw clenched.

Marcus turned and prayed no weapon would find his back as he closed the distance to the wall. After what felt like an eternity, he reached the fortifications and used the rope to climb back up.

'They are coming,' said Máedóc the moment Marcus swung his legs over the edge of the wall.

'The Northmen?' Marcus turned.

'No, the Irish prisoners. You did it. They released them.'

Fourteen figures ran across the grass towards the monastery. Behind them, the Northmen dismounted.

'They are getting ready to attack,' Marcus said.

'Donnchadh, bring the archers from the west wall and open the gate. Stop the Irish before they step on the caltrops and tell them to keep close to the wall. Close the gates as soon as they are inside!'

It pained Marcus that he was forced to weaken his defences just when the Northmen were about to attack. On the plains to the east, the heathens lined up in four units and spread out to attack from several angles at once. Two groups moved towards the east wall, while the two groups on the flanks went towards the gate to the south and the practically unmanned north wall.

Marcus ran north along the wall until he came to the groups guarding the east wall. The girl Betha and her family were among the eight frightened defenders.

'Come! Grab some stones and move to that platform over there.' Marcus pointed to an area on the north wall. 'We're getting reinforcements through the gates now, so we do not need that many people right here.' He patted Betha on the head and ran back.

The gates opened, and soon after, weeping women and children poured in, led by a novice. Eight men hurried to put the logs back in place to brace the gate. Donnchadh and Máedóc walked among the newly arrived Irish and tried to comfort them while equipping them with bows and spears. Marcus shook his head. None of them would offer any help repelling the attack that was coming.

'Archers, prepare! Everybody else: use the stones when they are just below you. Wait with the spears until they climb the wall! Hide behind the wall until they are almost there!' Marcus commanded as he darted between the groups.

Marcus heard the trampling feet of the Northmen charging towards the place where he was standing, and he grabbed a spear before he looked over the wall. Three dozen warriors were thirty steps away. Their round shields protecting their heads and upper bodies.

Twenty steps away.

'Wait,' he whispered to the archers next to him.

Ten steps.

'Get ready! Let loose at my command!'

The Irish got to their feet and found their marks.

The Northmen reached the sharpened pikes in front of the wall. Nobody impaled themselves, but the shield formations disintegrated as they climbed over the stakes. Two loud screams revealed that they had also found some of the caltrops scattered on the ground.

Marcus looked down again, raising his arm. Beneath him, he saw faces he knew well.

Magnus Trygg led the charge. Geir Galne jumped around on one foot while grabbing the other with both hands. And there was Bjarn.

Marcus lowered his arm.

'Shoot!'

CHAPTER 39: SENTENCE

The small church was packed, as usual. There were more people living in Woodhorn than the church was built to accommodate. The flow of desolate women and children from raided coastal villages like Wucestre had boosted the population. The grand Lord Edric sat in the front row with his family. Julia stood by the back wall with Esme, Mildred and Durwin. There was room for everybody in the house of the Lord, but that did not mean you would find a place to sit.

Somebody had lit the fireplace, even though it was spring, and it was already uncomfortably hot. Julia resented that the priest spoke terrible Latin and flattered Lord Edric on every occasion. She had thought about telling him that the Mongrel stole food from the miners, but she could not bring herself to do it. She did not trust this priest. If she could learn to set snares, they might survive without working in the mines. At least through the summer and autumn. If only the hopeless priest could be done with his mindless chatter. She smiled as the slender man closed the book in front of him and took a few steps forward.

'Matthew tells us that what comes out of the mouth comes from the heart, and it makes a man unclean. From the heart come evil thoughts, murder, adultery, theft and lies.'

The priest lowered his head in silent prayer before lifting his gaze once more.

'It pains me to tell you that among us there are children

with evil hearts, who steal, lie and threaten to murder good people!'

Gasps and murmurs sounded from the congregation. At once, everybody was awake and alert. A stark contrast to the drowsiness that accompanied the mumbling Latin sermon, which none of them understood.

'Julia of Wucestre. Step forward to be judged before the Lord!'

Julia looked around in horror. Not many people knew her, but some eyes were already on her. Lord Edric had turned to look for her. Two rows behind him sat the Mongrel, with his head lowered. Three grown men rose from the benches and came towards her.

The damned Mongrel had ratted on her!

After a glance at Esme, she hasted towards the aisle and rounded the corner towards the doors a few paces ahead of the men chasing her. With a glance backwards, Julia threw all caution to the wind and dashed.

Straight into the arms of two men guarding the door.

They grabbed her upper arms and they carried her to the altar while the priest preached about the absolution of sins in a shrill voice. Julia squirmed and thrashed until two other men grabbed her legs, holding her fast.

'Has the devil possessed you, girl?' asked the priest.

Julia understood her peril and managed to stop fighting. Life was short for those a priest had deemed possessed. As soon as she got her legs free, she fell to her knees in front of the priest with her head bowed. If she was to survive this, she would have to play her part well.

'No, Father. I was angry and scared because I have been accused of something I have not done.'

'Are you Julia of Wucestre?'

'Yes.'

'How old are you?'

'This was my fourteenth winter, Father.'

'Then you are old enough to be responsible for your sins!' declared the priest.

'Which sins, Father?'

'You have stolen the miners' bread, accused an honest man of stealing and threatened to kill the same man if he told somebody!'

'That's a lie!' Julia replied with more restraint than she felt. 'The Mongrel stole the bread instead of handing it out to the workers!'

'Quiet, girl! You cannot cover one sin with another! Do you bear false witness in the house of the Lord?'

'No, Father, I'm telling the truth.'

'Then you must prove your innocence or take your punishment!'

When Julia looked up, she realised how this trap worked. Two of the men who had picked her up came carrying a large iron pot hanging from a stick between them. She felt the heat as they placed it on the stone floor in front of her. That was why they had lit the fireplace. They had planned everything, and she had not sensed anything amiss.

'Julia of Wucestre. You claim to be falsely accused. As the Lord's servant on earth, I ask you to pick up the stone from the boiling water in front of you. If you are innocent, the Lord will see grace in you and protect you from the heat. In three days, you will show us your hands. If they are free from wounds, the Lord has healed you and confirmed your innocence. Then, you are free. However, should you still have wounds or blisters in three days, you are guilty and will be judged for your sins!'

Julia sat still as she thought it through. There was no way out of this. If she put her arms in the boiling water, the skin would be scald and blistered. It would hurt day and night, and if the wounds festered, she would die within a week. Nothing she had experienced in life gave her hope that God had any interest in sparing her, this day or any other day. The heathens had destroyed her home and family, and now a priest in the Lord's church was ready to sentence her to death for a sin he knew she had not committed.

If Esme or anyone else dared speak out to defend her, they would also be asked to put their arms in the hot water to prove that they spoke the truth. Nobody could save her.

'I confess my sins,' she said, her head bowed. 'I have borne evil in my heart, and my thoughts have been evil.'

The women at the back of the church gasped in terror. Julia heard some of the men laughing behind her. The Mongrel. Lord Edric. The priest. She hated them because they had tricked her. It would never happen again, that was for sure. Her heart filled with something warm and invigorating. Never again!

'She is guilty. Take her out!'

It was Lord Edric who spoke. Two of his men grabbed Julia and led her through the church. This time, she walked on her own accord.

Just outside the church, she was forced to her knees. The priest had done his part. Now it was the Lord's turn to judge her. Julia sat quietly while expectant churchgoers poured out and filled the space in front of her. Relieved, she noticed that Esme was leading the children home. At least they would not have to see what was about to happen.

'Julia of Wucestre,' cried Lord Edric. 'You have confessed to stealing a loaf of bread and trying to blame another. As King Aethelred's trusted man and deputy in Woodhorn, it is my duty to judge you in the presence of the Lord. Do you have anything to add before I proclaim your sentence?'

'Only the Lord's words from the Proverbs,' Julia replied. 'A false witness will not go unpunished, and he who utters lies will not escape.'

It was something her mother used to say, to teach her children not to lie. But this day, it meant more. Julia lowered her head and closed her eyes.

A moment of silence followed.

'Well spoken, girl,' said Lord Edric, at last, revealing that he had not noticed the threat. 'It is to your benefit that you confess your sins and turn to God in this moment of shame. Therefore, your life will be spared.'

There was a chorus of disappointed sighs from the crowd. Julia found no reason to rejoice at Edric's generosity. It was not common to be sentenced to death for stealing a loaf of bread, so she had not feared it. More often, the thief had to pay with a few fingers, or ...

'For your sinful deeds, you shall pay with your left ear!' cried Lord Edric.

The congregation cheered. Cutting off an ear was not great entertainment, but the one who had lost an ear would bear the visible shame every day for the rest of her life, no matter where she was. Always a thief, always an outsider, always of lesser worth. There was little in life that pleased a Christian as much as feeling better than his neighbour.

Julia remained calm and still until the cold blade began to separate her ear from her head.

CHAPTER 40: INSIDE

Ulv kept his head down as he entered the gate alongside the last group of Irish captives Kjetil Jarl had released, primarily women and children. He hoped that nobody would look closely at the hostages. Ulv's disguise was dubious. When the opportunity arose, he hastily draped his cloak over the monk's robes Bjarn had given him.

Fortunately, the cries of alarm sounded as soon as they were inside the walls. Of course, Kjetil took advantage of the minor distraction to storm the monastery.

Children screamed in terror, and the frightened and confused adults could not offer much consolation. Their situation was terrible, and their prospects were grim. Only a handful of monks stood between them and a host of Vikings under the leadership of a wicked Jarl.

Among the new arrivals, there was one man who kept his composure, and Ulv followed him with his gaze until he disappeared into the monastery yard. Ulv started after him but halted when a monk grabbed his shoulder and held out a spear for him. In his other hand, he held a bow and some arrows, and Ulv reached out for those instead. Their eyes met for a moment, and the monk froze.

A stream of arbitrary alternatives flowed through Ulv's mind. Should he pull his seax and kill the monk? That would expose him the moment the gate closed. Could he disable the monk with a clenched fist or strangle him? The outcome would be the same as if he drew his seax. His options were limited, and all were unpleasant. Ulv tried to smile.

Another outcry broke the tension. Above them, a young monk shouted commands as he ran along the walls.

Marcus!

Without a word, the monk handed Ulv the bow and rushed to help his brothers reinforce the gates with logs. Ulv briefly examined the short bow before retreating into the monastery courtyard and found his way to a small building some distance from the walls. Out of sight, he removed his cloak. With the monk's robes and the grey hood pulled over his head, he stepped outside once more to get an overview of the surroundings.

The monks had built platforms along the walls, where groups of archers were free to shoot at oncoming Northmen. The two towers in the southern corners appeared to be weakly defended by a handful of Irish peasants.

Ulv found Marcus again, looking over the edge of the wall from a platform, with one hand up in the air. Archers stood ready, waiting for his orders. The merchant's son and former thrall had become a monk and an army commander. Ulv's friend was now his enemy. What would come next?

Ulv had to get hold of Marcus alone, but how? He looked around once more. Behind him was a tower, manned by two archers, with a door at ground level. To his right, a warrior in wolf furs had scaled the wall and was confronted by a monk and two peasants. Most people would be at a disadvantage against three foes, but the agile wolfskin seemed undaunted by the challenge. It was Vass!

The battle would soon be over. Kjetil's warriors would exploit the weakness caused by Vass's attack, and once the Northmen were inside, the Irish would not last long.

Ulv headed for the tower door. He was running out of time.

CHAPTER 41: REUNION

Three defenders engaged Vass when he reached the top of the wall. To his left was a monk with a simple spear. The two men to his right appeared more accustomed to weapons. One held a large woodsman's axe in both hands, and the man behind him wielded a spear. The axeman advanced with caution. Too much caution, considering they were three against one. Their best chance was to charge at the same time. The monk on the left shouted, took two steps forward and thrust with his spear. Vass angled his shield, and the spear slid harmlessly to the side. As the brave monk drove forward, the wolfskin slammed his shield against the upper body of the wide-eyed foe.

With an 'Ooofff', the monk tumbled off the platform.

The axeman used the distraction to attack. He was fast, but not fast enough. Vass parried the wild, vertical swing and deflected the axe up and to the side. The axeman overbalanced, as inexperienced axe wielders often did when they missed a swing. Vass turned his body, leading with the shield, and drove the boss into his opponent's face. The Irishman dropped his axe and slumped.

The spearman timed his attack better and stabbed over the body of his fallen companion. Vass stepped back with his left foot and spun away from the weapon. Completing the pirouette, he came around with his shield first. The shield pushed away the spear, and the sword slashed into the man's neck. The fight was over in less than ten heartbeats.

Vass pulled his sword free while two Northmen scaled the wall behind him. Lifting his gaze, he noticed a familiar figure sneaking behind the tower he had seen Ulv approaching as he climbed the wall.

Vass jumped down from the platform and sprinted towards the tower.

He rounded the corner and shouted out to Ulv. The young man in monk's robes turned, and his eyes widened. Vass winced. Ulv threw himself backwards and barely managed to evade the attack from the man who had snuck up on him. When his backstab failed, the enemy sidestepped to ensure he did not get caught between Vass and Ulv.

'Finn,' said Ulv.

Finn backed slowly as his gaze moved between the two Vikings.

'Do what you have to do, Ulv. I'll take care of this,' said Vass.

Ulv nodded and disappeared through the tower door.

CHAPTER 42: NIGHT

Hiding in the mine after sunset was easy. Julia helped the last kids up the ropes before she pulled back against a wall and waited. She rubbed her face and hands with coal dust as if the dirt from a day's work was not enough. Her clothes were filthier than usual, as she had not washed them since she lost her ear.

The light in the shaft faded to a barely visible grey haze in the dim starlight. It was time to act. Julia's eyes had become accustomed to the darkness and found the ropes. After the climb, she lay still on the ground and breathed in the mild spring air. The village slept under a moonless sky.

She slipped out to the edge of the forest and found the bundle she had hidden under a root the night before. The forest had been her home after she had persuaded Esme to take the children south to Eoforwic and look for work there. They would not suffer the consequences for what Julia was about to do.

Julia unfolded the blanket and spread the contents on the grass. After folding the blanket lengthwise a couple of times, she hung it around her neck and fastened it with her belt rope. Although it was a bit bulky, she would need the blanket on cold nights. At her right hip hung a knife, and on the other side, she carried her father's sword. The blade was still dull and wrapped in cloth. Soon, she would have plenty of time on her own and could polish it until it was shiny and sharp. This night, the knife had to do the job. The only thing left was a leather purse with the flint, steel and whetstone Cwen had given her. She attached it to her belt. Those items were everything she owned and everything she needed.

Another coughing fit shook her body, but pressing the blanket over her mouth, she muffled the sounds. She wiped her mouth and started back towards the buildings. Passing the mines, she followed the route she had taken every night after sunset – the road to the Mongrel's house.

The sounds from inside made her sit down and wait in the dark. The Mongrel had company, again. But as before, the young girl soon left with a piece of bread in her hand. Some earn a living by working from sunrise to sunset. For others, their workday begins after sunset. The girl had to find a new job tomorrow.

Soon, Julia stood over the Mongrel and watched him while he slept. It was so easy, and it felt so right. The Mongrel woke abruptly when the sharp knife opened his throat, and he grabbed her as the blood pumped out of his body with each heartbeat. Julia let him hold her. It did not matter. He would soon be dead. Very soon. His upper body fell to the floor. The smell of his blood and her vomit filled the room.

Julia turned to leave but realised that the girl would be blamed for the murder. She had been the last one here, and Lord Edric would not hesitate to sacrifice another poor young girl. No, she would not let that happen.

With the bloody knife, she cut an ear off the corpse and pressed it into his hand. Julia of Wucestre, the priest and Lord Edric had called her, before they cut off her ear. Everybody would know it was her, and nobody else would be blamed for the murder. The murders. That was how it had to be.

Her eyes filled with tears as she left the tiny house and walked in the direction of the church. Not because she was sad, as she felt no grief over the Mongrel's death. Something in her had changed. It was as if the ice was melting. Her fears were gone. All ties were cut. Nobody could ever judge her or discipline her again. She had defeated an enemy who wanted her dead, and she had regained the power over her own life. Her hands trembled, but her chest was filled with warmth. There were two enemies left until she was free.

To avoid the light from the oil lamps hanging by the church gate, she walked in a wide arc until she came to the back of Lord Edric's manor.

The walls were built of stone, not of wicker branches like most other buildings in the village. The house was larger than the others, but it was round with a hay roof like the rest. A wooden door covered the only opening in the stone wall. Julia stood in the dark, thinking about how to get in unnoticed. The lord had a wife and children. She had seen that when they sat on the front bench in the church. There could be no witnesses to what she was about to do.

Her gaze went to the oil lamps hanging outside the church gate. They swayed gently in the night breeze. If she set the roof on fire, the family would come running out. Then she could get to Edric without any of the kids getting in her way. But by then, the rest of the inhabitants of Woodhorn would also gather to put out the fire and prevent it from spreading. They may even start looking for an arsonist. Some might suggest that they look for her, because she would always be the culprit here in Woodhorn. The fingers of her left hand touched the band tied around her head to protect the wound where her ear had been.

Julia stalked towards the house and pulled the door. Before it had moved a finger's width, it made a creaking sound from the top corner. Julia kept the door still until she was sure nobody had woken up and made another attempt. The door opened a little more and made a sound that was almost similar to the previous one. The opening was large enough for Julia to get her hand in. Little by little, she slipped the door open until she managed to squeeze inside. There were no light sources inside, so Julia stood still until she could make out the layout of the room. It was too dark to discern any details, but she got an impression of where the walls and the largest pieces of furniture stood. Her uncovered right ear helped her locate Lord

Edric. With the knife in hand, she padded in the direction of the loudest sound of breathing until she stood in front of the large bed where Edric and his wife slept.

Between them lay a child.

Julia froze with the knife blade a handsbreadth from Lord Edric's bare neck. A quick movement of her wrist and the man who sentenced her to a life of shame would bleed to death in his bed.

In front of the eyes of his wife and children.

Their lives would be ruined, just as the Vikings had ruined hers.

She retreated to the door and squeezed out. Leaning against the stone wall, she listened for sounds from within. Silence. The creaking door did not wake anyone this time either.

Weary, she looked at the nearby church. Where the priest lay sleeping, alone and unprotected. It would be easy to take her revenge on him. She had fantasised about pouring boiling water all over his body so he could ask the Lord to heal the wounds in three days. It had felt so good thinking about it, but now she felt nothing. What would it achieve? Another priest would just replace him with the same convictions. The same sins. The same evil.

Her gaze fell on the oil lamps. To the final end of Woodhorn's mining operations. If she let a lit oil lamp down the shaft, it would break, and all the oil would catch fire simultaneously. It would ignite the treacherous mining air from the tunnels, and the entire mine would be destroyed in a tremendous roar. The kids who worked underground would not have to crawl around in the dark from sunrise to sunset for an onion and a small piece of bread. They would be free.

Free to do what?

The very next day, they would miss the little food they had been given and would have to find other ways to feed themselves. Worse ways, for some. For most of them.

Julia made up her mind and started walking under the dim light of the stars. The mines in Woodhorn had kept her alive through the winter. Now she was marked as a thief and could never expect help from anyone. Before the first frost came, she had to learn all she needed to fend for herself next winter.

She returned to the marshes.

Back to Cwen.

CHAPTER 43: LOSS

Ulv's heart pounded, and his hands trembled. If Vass had arrived a moment later, Ulv would have been dead. He never knew the lethal Irishman was behind him. It was him, Finn, who had entered through the gates with the women and children and disappeared into the courtyard. Ulv took a deep breath and picked up the bow and the five arrows. With the seax in his right hand and the bow in his left, he started up the stairs.

There were two archers on the roof. One stood to the left and faced the eastern wall, where Vass had made an opening for the attackers. The other had an arrow pointing towards the monastery courtyard.

Ulv laid down bow and arrows and stalked towards the man on the left. Behind him, he changed his grip on the large knife and struck the pommel against the back of the man's head. The Irishman fell to the ground. Ulv turned in time to see the other archer swirl around with an arrow on the string. An experienced bowman would not hesitate in such a situation, and Ulv expected that the arrow was on its way. He threw himself forward, curled up and rolled. He was rewarded with the sound of an arrow bouncing off the stone floor.

When Ulv got to his feet a few steps from the archer, the Irishman dropped his bow and drew his knife. Ulv dived forward and stabbed him in the stomach. The man howled and clutched his wound. Ulv tossed away the man's knife, grabbed his legs and toppled him, screaming over the edge.

Ulv turned to the scene below, where Marcus had stopped in the middle of an order and turned to the sound of the man thumping to the ground. The merchant's son gaze followed the tower up to the top. His eyes found Ulv.

Ulv pulled off the hood of his grey robe.

They stood staring at each other, as if in the eye of the storm, while the world raged around.

Suddenly, Marcus sped off towards the tower. Ulv walked to the trap door in the floor. With the blood-dripping knife in his hand, he waited for the thrall, the monk, the commander. His friend and his enemy.

Marcus came up on the roof, carrying a spear. His angry expression posed the unspoken question: *Why are you here?*

Ulv had to concentrate on not lifting the knife. Instead, he spoke. They did not have much time.

'Marcus, the battle is lost. We are already within the walls. Vass is inside. And soon, there will be many more. It is over. You have to save yourself ...'

'Save myself?' Marcus interrupted. 'Become your slave, you mean? Save myself for a life as a thrall? A slave to those who killed my mother, my sister, my father. To the man who killed my father. Is that how I'm going to save myself?'

'There are worse alternatives, Marcus. Believe me.'

Marcus just stared at him. His body trembled with emotion and blood lust. He would not be easily persuaded.

'We can run, Marcus. If we do it right now, we have a chance. To live. To have a life. A choice. If we hesitate ... If you stay here ...'

Ulv shook his head. Marcus was still staring at him with clenched teeth.

'Kjetil is down there. The moment he comes in, you're dead. You know that,' said Ulv.

'I've made a deal with Flatnose,' Marcus replied, but he did not seem convinced.

Ulv only raised his eyebrows.

Suddenly, a roar erupted from the opening in the floor. They both turned to see Geir Galne climbing up with a knife in his hand. He somehow limped on both feet, and a broken arrow protruded from his thigh. His face was a grimace of madness and rage. Ulv had seen Galne out of control before, but this was something else. And much worse. The saliva hung from his mouth, and the entire upper body of the tall warrior was stained with blood.

'You ugly, spit-licking White Christ whore, I will bite off your sweaty ears and stuff them down your throat!' Galne snarled.

Marcus shouted and stabbed the spear at the berserk, who came plunging forward on shaky legs. Ulv admired the young monk's determination. A reckless attack might be his only hope.

But Geir Galne had fought dozens, perhaps hundreds, of battles. And doubtless many in this state of blind aggression. Injured and hampered.

Galne grabbed the spear, pulled it sideways and met Marcus by driving his forehead into the young man's face. Marcus fell and clutched his head, but no sound or scream escaped him. The berserk was over him with a knife to his face.

If Ulv was going to save Marcus, he had to do it now. He advanced a step, then another, and another, until he stood over the fuming berserk who screamed at Marcus and pressed a knife against his throat. Ulv inhaled and stabbed his seax against Geir Galne's back.

Galne spun around with impossible speed. With his left hand, he slapped the knife out of Ulv's hand. The right hand followed with a blow to Ulv's chin. Ulv fell to the ground, and his hands went to his neck. He expected to feel the blood gushing out, but the berserk had struck with his fist with the knife pointing to the side. His head spun, and the world became a blur. Ulv turned his head to see Galne bent over Marcus once more. The hoarse voice hissed:

‘You will look me in the eyes while your life goes out of you, you little … you little …’

Everything went slower for Ulv. He could not keep his eyes open. A horn sounded in the distance, then another. Geir Galne swore.

The world disappeared.

***

The story continues in

*- **Free** -*

Printed in Great Britain
by Amazon

48081744R00136